THE POWER OF WEAKNESS

Other books in the 2X2 series:

Here and Somewhere Else
Grace Paley and Robert Nichols

The Riddle of Life and Death
Tillie Olsen and Leo Tolstoy

To Stir the Heart
Bessie Head and Ngugi wa Thiong'o

THE POWER OF WEAKNESS

—

DING LING AND
LU HSUN

WITH AN INTRODUCTION BY
TANI E. BARLOW

The Feminist Press
at the City University of New York
New York

Published in 2007 by The Feminist Press at the City University of New York,
The Graduate Center, 365 Fifth Avenue, Suite 5406, New York, NY 10016

Library of Congress Cataloging-in-Publication Data

Ling, Ding, 1904-1985
 [Selections. English. 2007]
 The power of weakness / [selected works of Ding Ling and Lu Hsun [Xun] ;
with an Introduction by Tani E. Barlow. -- 1st ed.
    p. cm. -- (2 x 2 series)
 ISBN-13: 978-1-55861-548-9 (pbk. : alk. paper)
 ISBN-10: 1-55861-548-2 (pbk. : alk. paper)
 1. Lu Hsun [Xun], 1881-1936--Translations into English. 2. Ding, Ling,
1904---Translations into English. I. Ding, Ling, English. 1904-
Selections. 2007. II. Title.
 PL2754.S5A23 2007
 895.1'35--dc22

                              2006101584

Text and cover design by Lisa Force
Printed in Canada

13 12 11 10 09 08 07   5 4 3 2 1

CONTENTS

—

INTRODUCTION

How do you write about a revolution? Predictably readers turn to memoirs for the answer. Stories about personal or catastrophic family experiences, shaped to suit the political tastes of North American readers, and novels about the forced migration of foremothers in delicate tales like *The Joy Luck Club* or other novels of Chinese wartime catastrophes convey a sense of how revolution was lived. They give retrospective assurance. Leavened with literary nostalgia, tales particularly of revolutionary violence, recalled through the ruinous hurt that teenage experience enshrines in memory, give us a sense of having been present at a traumatic event and surviving it. Perhaps readers devour memoirs and novels because they combine first-person reporting with narrative reconstruction and assurance that the revolution is definitively over. They reestablish distance while retaining the illusion of immediacy.

My question is more intimate and more practical. It haunts the work of revolutionary and counterrevolutionary writers alike and it is more like: *How do I write about the revolution I am living?* When The Feminist Press invited me to comment on a volume of canonical revolutionary writing by twentieth-century literary figures Lu Hsun and Ding Ling, I agreed precisely because they were great revolutionary writers, bent on inventing literary techniques that could put into words the experiences they were living. Warning: these writers were not "nice" people. They were weak though sometimes strong; they were alternately cynical and gullible; sometimes they were passionate, determined, generous, sometimes spiteful, and in the case of Ding Ling who outlived Lu Hsun by fifty years, perhaps as much victimizer as victim. Ignoring their outsized personalities for the moment, I believe their literature moves away from the conventional problems of memoir, history, or film and toward a more ambiguous problem: understanding how Chinese revolutionary writers survived and navigated their times, in fits of elation and generosity or fearful disavowal, sometimes brutally, cynically, manipulatively, or punitively, and always with the sanctimony of revolutionary moralists.

Lu Hsun and Ding Ling wrote the revolution in the moment, as it unfolded. For that reason, and since the revolutionary writer is politically engaged, their fiction places a premium on change, on renovation. Consequently their fiction seems insatiable. It never stops asking, "When?" For instance, buried in the bleakest of accounts told by a priggish, young, alienated protagonist of a Lu Hsun story or the subjectivist laments of any of Ding Ling's modern "girls," there is always aching disquiet and the implicit question, When will the current ugly present yield to a better future? This is a progressive form of fiction. So in it nothing is ever resolved definitively. Written ferociously in the moment, the stories and essays are propulsive and abrasive; literary works in motion, they cannot serve as still mirrors on a settled past.

So although we may have to abandon certainty about historical fact when we are reading these stories, we also gain something from the writers' ambivalence. Set ideas—free-choice marriage is modern, arranged marriage is tradition; individualism is modern, collectivism is tradition—do appear in these stories and many others that these great writers published. Yet much as the old is attacked here, the new or modern cannot be embraced because the modern, too, is profoundly unjust. Maybe, these writers suggest, what passes for modern life is not much of an improvement on the so-called tradition it seeks to displace. In other words, often so-called modern and so-called tradition merge in revolutionary fiction. What we sense more than the orderly march of time from tradition to modernity is a special urgency in the revolutionist's writing. *How is it possible to fold an immediate moment of injustice into an appropriate literary form?* Readers may be better off abandoning the effort to declare some things "traditional" and others squarely "modern."

Acknowledging the importance of writing about the revolution that you are living helps us to grasp why Lu Hsun insisted that his writing came from daily life affairs. He could not, he claimed, know truth from the outside. Not for him

3

was the omniscient novel written from the point of view of a god or historian, since he could not pretend to know how things really were or how they would turn out in the end. So Lu Hsun conveyed truth from the perspective of everyday experience. He might write an essay attacking an intellectual charlatan and publish it in a daily paper. Or, in despair about political events, he might rewrite an old story employing ambiguous contemporary language. A meditation about the national identity of the writer's own moustache, or a pointed political attack on his old friend Lin Yutang over the politics at stake in humorous writing, it did not matter. Over time and in his efforts to write in the moment, Lu Hsun honed a modernist literary form, the *zawen*, which are satiric, critical essays. That was not the only thing Lu Hsun invented. To write about revolution—the liberation of women, children's emancipation, diagnosing the corrupt national character, the importance of good fatherhood, extending citizenship, abolishing cruel customary practices, cultural revolution—in immediate terms, Lu Hsun found it necessary to recreate narrative forms for literary expression, too. But the *zawen* is a good example of how the exigencies of revolution propelled writers to remake literary convention.

Like Lu Hsun, Ding Ling also drew on things she saw and heard, building from the gossipy details of everyday life. But when, in 1941, Ding Ling decided to publish a critique of the Communist Party's political strategy for women's lib-eration, she wrote in the genre of Lu Hsun's *zawen*. In other words, what the older writer adapted to capture the revolu-

4

tion he was living, the younger one used to intervene in a revolutionary policy debate at a moment of war planning.

As readers we cannot blink in the face of the immediacy these writers lived. Whether under house arrest, enduring brutal political censorship, eking out a poor living as editor or translator, or living high on the hog, the darling of readers shackled to an official state literary organizations, Lu Hsun and Ding Ling found ways to write their urgently lived moments. Between them these two writers produced some of the most recognizable twentieth-century colloquial Chinese short stories ever written.

Renowned as a founder of the Chinese modernist literary canon, Lu Hsun's "New Year Sacrifice" (1924) and "Regret for the Past" (1926) collected here are stories about the suffering of women related to the reader by a third person, a repellent, internally conflicted male narrator. Ding Ling launched the tradition of women's self-narrated fiction and, later, pioneered Chinese conventions for writing socialist realist fiction. She, too, altered the Chinese language of literary expression. What we also see in Ding Ling's "New Faith" (1939) and "When I was in Xia Village" (1941) is an assertion, even a ludicrous insistence, that although the social beatings women take—commonly about sexual matters—is harsh, women survive them.

Lu Hsun (also known as Lu Xun)[1] is the pen name of Zhou Shuren, born September 25, 1881. His reputable gentry household consisted of a nationally ranked scholar, his grandfather;

a man who had achieved the primary degree in the national examinations, his father; a rural woman named Zhou Rui, his mother, who had taught herself to read; Ah Chang, Shuren's superstitious woman servant; and three younger brothers. One of the brothers, Zhou Zuoren, became a celebrated writer, particularly associated with Japanese cultural politics in Chinese intellectual circles. Another, Zhou Jianren, pioneered the study of eugenics and evolutionary theory and rose within the Communist bureaucracy before the Cultural Revolution. The third brother died in childhood. For much of his short life, Lu Hsun looked after this extended household, supporting family members and shepherding the family finances.

After an idyllic early education in the old tutorial, small school fashion, a decline in family fortunes and the death of his father led Lu Hsun to enroll in the Jiangnan Naval Academy and then to transfer to the School of Mines and Railways. There he studied science, German, and English. He also encountered Yan Fu's translation of Huxley's *Evolution and Ethics* and the reformist journal *Shiwu bao*, edited by pioneer revolutionary Liang Qiqiao. In 1902 Lu Hsun went to Japan on a government scholarship, spending seven years there before returning home with expertise in Japanese, European languages, new philosophy, and a political perspective honed by years inside the Chinese progressive community in Japan. Lu Hsun spent the first three years back home living from job to job on the strength of old school ties and, following the Revolution of 1911, writing short stories as he taught, edited, and translated to secure his livelihood. As a returned student from abroad, he finally got a government sinecure, which allowed him access to cultural preservation circles and exposure to new trends in the visual arts. The years he spent as a nominal official of the Ministry of Education in Beijing are said to have been years of personal depression. Yet, despite this handicap, those years from 1912 to 1926 were the ones in which he produced some of his best-known literature, established himself as a college teacher, editor, translator, and cultural commentator. He assiduously cared for the woman his parents had married to him (though historians claim the marriage was never consummated), and fell in love with Xu Guangping, a former student who became Lu Hsun's life companion, secretary, and the mother of their only child.

In the explosive years between the White Terror of 1927, in which the GMD or Nationalist Party purged Communists from its cadre corps and set up murderous anti-Communist policies, and his death from tuberculosis on October 6, 1936, Lu Hsun's political stance hardened and sharpened. He lived intensely in Shanghai with close collaborators and major interlocutors—his brother Zhou Jianren and Jianren's wife Wang Yunru; writer Yu Dafu; ultra-leftist writer-activists Mao Dun, Feng Xuefeng, and Rou Shi (whom the GMD government executed along with Ding Ling's lover Hu Ye-pin in 1931; Communist theorists Qu Qiubai and Hu Feng.) And during his Shanghai years for the first time he supported himself and his extended family exclusively through his writing. Lu Hsun's motives for aligning himself with the Communist movement ranged from the example of his lover Xu Guangping's activism, to the worsening political climate, to his cumulative, pessimistic view of the corrupt "modern" society of the Republican GMD government, and to a late-blooming ardor for partisanship on behalf of the truly wretched of the earth. He protected and mentored young writers. Dressed in his characteristic uniform of a long black gown and black tennis shoes, cultural revolutionary Lu Hsun engaged in political activities organized by the Chinese Communist Party (CCP) apparatus. He was active at the leadership level in the League of Left Wing Writers, established in the early 1930s, and participated in the factionalizing debates that quickly polarized left-wing literary circles in Shanghai. Bitter debates led the CCP leadership to shut down the League in 1936, but not before two hostile camps had coalesced, which would, by the early forties, result in renewed hostility between the Lu Hsun Academy faction headed by Zhou Yang and the Society for Literary Resistance, which Ding Ling allegedly headed.

Ding Ling is the pen name of Jiang Bingzhi. Born a generation later than Lu Hsun, in 1904, she was the elder daughter of a remarkable woman, a widow named Yu Manzhen, whose husband had come from a large, rich, provincial family in Hunan. Like other privileged, revolutionary women, including later Communist Party theorist Xiang Jingyu, Manzhen learned mathematics, science, geography, and rights theory and thus prepared herself to teach in the new girls' schools set up in the declining years of the old dynasty. Once her Japan-educated husband had died, Manzhen struck out on her own. She set an example of militancy in street demonstrations, in her mode of thinking, and in her disciplined insistence on women's economic self-sufficiency. Following in her mother's footsteps but against her mother's advice, Ding Ling quit formal education early and fled Changsha, Hunan, for the life of a cultural revolutionary and anarchist itinerant in Nanjing, Beijing, and Shanghai. As part of her teenage life of self-willed freedom, Ding Ling formed passionate attachments to friends, male and female, seeming, one biographer has suggested, to fall in love hastily and repeatedly. Like other cultural revolutionaries, Ding Ling was expressing in social-political action the big ideas of the so-called Chinese New Culture Movement (circa 1915) and the May Fourth movement (circa 1919). Among these were the right to love, the right to control one's body, and the belief that female cupidity and libido are positive evolutionary forces. Militant youths believed that in the act of love and by repudiating the Chinese big family "system" they could transform the rotten society that Lu Hsun was describing in groundbreaking stories like "Soap."

Like Lu Hsun, therefore, Ding Ling belonged to an aristocracy of progressive Chinese intellectuals. Her early exposure to female educational institutions, in which she spent her childhood, actually ensured that she, like Lu Hsun, belonged to this elite new intellectual class. Through the set of connections that stretched out of elite girls' schools, including her alma mater Changsha Girls School, the Common Girls School of Shanghai and Shanghai University, where Qu Qiubai helped to found the modern discipline of sociology, through early anarchist- and Communist-organizing groups, Ding Ling could count as friends or lovers most of Lu Hsun's social circle. Communist Party Secretary, sociologist, and poet Qu Qiubai; the literary muse and modern "girl" Wang Jianhong; Marxist theorist Xiang Jingyu; proletarian writer Hu Yepin; translator Feng Da; theorist and critic Feng Xuefeng—all either knew her from childhood or had encountered the short, vivacious, emotional young woman whose personality struck some as artless and others as histrionic.

It was from among these giants of revolutionary cultural life that Ding Ling sought not only lovers but readers, too. A young dilettante, she finally settled on writing as a vocation and produced in a spurt of remarkable creativity the foundational texts of what became Chinese women's modernist writing. Diffident, female, in a world that had yet to recognize a comfortable resolution to the challenge that being a famous woman writer presented, Ding Ling, like Lu Hsun, hesitated initially. But when her partner Hu Yepin's underground Communist work led to his execution, Ding Ling, too, stepped into formal political commitment and, thus, into outlaw status. She was consequently targeted by the GMD apparatus, kidnapped, and subjected to a campaign of persuasion since all sides in the struggle during these years recognized the important influence of leading intellectual revolutionaries on the young people who consumed their literature. Her ambivalence and the child she conceived with a lover who had betrayed her put a permanent "black mark" on Ding Ling's revolutionary record.

After Ding Ling fled captivity she surfaced in the Red Army camp at Yan'an. The citizens of this new world were soldiers, refugees, migrant scholars from the cities, rural elites, and endless numbers of farmers: poor, poorer, and utterly impoverished. To write the revolution at the level of the everyday became her literary objective, which put her in the camp of the Maoists. Like Mao Zedong, she embraced and idealized this harsh world of rural poverty, seeking methods of representation—generic forms deemed appropriate for expressing the rural everyday as a romantic possibility. Romantic realism, the idealization of the potential of the poor to transform modern life and make it deliver on its promise to all, not just the lucky few, was Ding Ling's solution. In the end, after disciplinary action against her decision to publish "Thoughts on March 8," Ding Ling resurfaced, published her novel of Communist land reform and accompanied the new government to Beijing after their victory in the civil war. Not even a decade later, Ding Ling's faction lost badly in bureaucratic infighting and so, in 1958, she was expelled from privilege into the gulag. Until the mid-1970s the once celebrated writer lived below the line of sight, victim of crudely sexist slander against her romantic life. She suffered the machinations of intransigent enemies whose capacity for vengeful politics exceeded her own and in circumstances that went from uncomfortable to dire during the Cultural

Revolutionary decade, 1966-76. Ding Ling's final years were taken up with clearing her record for posterity. Critical opinion has not been kind to her proletarianized literature. Her status as a native daughter, however, has risen steadily among non-elite readers, among whom she is celebrated as writer and feminist.

Lu Hsun and Ding Ling were global writers. Each came to represent modern Chinese writing to worlds of readers outside of China, and both of them, perhaps Lu Hsun in a more scholarly and systematic fashion, wired themselves into the internationalist world of left-wing letters. By virtue of his international profile, in 1927 Lu Hsun was already being proposed as a candidate for the Nobel Prize. Though Ding Ling has always seemed a "native daughter" in comparison to the foreign-educated Lu Hsun, she was neither an unworldly nor a nativist figure. Agnes Smedley, journalist and militant, propagandized Ding Ling's profile and, as a fellow traveler Smedley moved with ease throughout the Communist world. Earl Leaf, Nym Wales, Edgar Snow, and other American journalists and advocates also interviewed Ding Ling at crucial times in her career, boosting her recognition in Anglophone circles. The constant flow of Chinese intellectual leftists like Qu Qiubai in and out of Moscow for training, education, rest, and rehabilitation also brought Eastern European and Russian cultural ideas into the world of writers, even ones like Ding Ling who had not yet traveled outside China and who neither read nor spoke a second language.

Of course, the revolutionary internationalism of these years depended on the work of translators everywhere. Lu Hsun translated widely from German, Japanese, and other languages into Chinese. He lived inside a flow of avant-garde international cultural and literary trends, and regularly patronized Uchiyama Kanzo's legendary Uchiyama Bookstore in Shanghai. There Japanese-literate Chinese intellectuals like Lu Hsun and his brothers bought access to the cosmopolitan world of Japanese language translations of world literature and philosophy.

But translation was only one aspect of the international exchange of ideas, trends, political practices, aesthetic theories, and literary influences. Given the established internationalism of left-wing Chinese letters, when on March 30, 1931, the GMD shot to death five writers, including Ruo Shi, confidant of Lu Hsun, and Lu Hsun's friend Hu Yepin, father of Ding Ling's son, the news was immediately flashed around the world to English, Japanese, Russian, French, and German progressives and media outlets. The International Union of Revolutionary Writers, Americans Jacob Lawrence and Upton Sinclair as well as Russian Stalinist Alexander Fadeyev issued a statement rebuking the government of China for its criminality.

Ding Ling and Lu Hsun became major Chinese cultural icons in part because they were awash in international revolutionary theory, literary trends, psychology, cultural politics, and Marxist aesthetic philosophy. During her time as senior editor of the League of Left Wing Writers' most successful literary journal ever, *Great Dipper*, Ding Ling and other League members, including comrades Qu Qiubai and Feng Xuefeng, actively promoted Marxist aesthetics, theories of proletarian culture, and debates about writing and representation, and struggled hard before the journal was banned to encourage an internationalist Chinese reading and writing culture. Of course *Great Dipper* was a front journal. Though not yet a CCP party member, Ding Ling was a de facto party operative. But that is precisely the point. In her policies of publishing new exploratory works by writers like poet Ai Qing, educated in France and influenced by Mayakovsky, and important writers in the tradition of Chinese women's fiction like Chen Hengzhe, the American-educated poet and professor, Ding Ling, like Lu Hsun (who apparently never joined the CCP), used *Dipper* and all the media at her disposal to organize intellectual commitments already cosmopolitan and internationalized.

Lu Hsun and Ding Ling became national icons, to be sure. Like W.E.B Dubois or Paul Robeson they were internationalists who represented "their" nation; ambassadors to the world from a homeland, citizens of a multicultural world. Since we tend to pigeonhole Ding Ling as Chinese and make Tillie Olsen all about the U.S. white working class, it is not surprising that these writers were bound together as internationalists and Communists. A similarity of ideas gave Ding Ling a lot in common with Alexandra Kollantai or Emma Goldman, Christa Wolf, and Doris Lessing. It is important to keep in mind the heterogeneous quality of international intellectual life in the nineteen thirties. This does nothing to deny the importance of national traditions. Over the last few years academic historians have disclosed that Lu Hsun's most significant work drew heavily on "traditional" literary conventions and narrative forms. That Lu Hsun's work is in some degree *neo*-traditionalist is beyond dispute. But no matter how indebted to the past even Lu Hsun's most experimental writing turns out to have been, there is no doubt that his perspective and the political concerns that saturate his work and Ding Ling's are part of international intellectual history.

Lu Hsun and Ding Ling were both proponents of women's liberation. They shared different positions with a common vision of progressive feminism enshrined in China and progressive circles everywhere. Each writer shared a debt to development philosophy that by Ding Ling's time had become a largely unquestioned element of modern thinking. The taproot of progressive feminism is Social Darwinian evolutionary theory. Chinese scholars of Lu Hsun's father's generation and his own had translated into Chinese key modernist theories of human life and society. The most pervasively influential were evolutionary theorists and among these the hands-down favorites were Thomas Huxley and Herbert Spencer; and for the young Lu Hsun, Ernest Haeckel as well. This is significant because Haeckel interpreted social evolution as a crudely racial struggle of the fittest. This presented Lu Hsun, who seems to have read Haeckel in Japanese, with a dilemma. He could not adopt a racialist theory that derogated the Asian. Yet, Haeckel provided him with a way of fashioning his characteristic self-critical views. In his thinking and literary imagination an internal debate over national character unfolds that obliquely borrows from a European perspective on and theory of civilization. The specter of race war made Lu Hsun hypercritical of the alleged failings of the Chinese as a people. Why are Chinese so cruel to each other, he asked? Isn't the Chinese patriarchy bizarrely abusive to children and women? Why are outdated patriarchal prejudices so deeply engrained in the everyday life of the people? Why do Chinese cling to defunct, hypocritical folkways that are, in naturalist terms, actually devolutionary? Lu Hsun asked such questions because, like Haeckel, he felt the progressivists' optimism drawn from the great tradition of evolutionary and social science progressive thinking.

These big social evolutionary ideas—eugenics and feminism—pervaded Chinese letters and consequently suffused the perspective of fiction writers who depicted everyday life in their stories. (Lest anyone think that Chinese intellectuals were fools to embrace eugenic racial theory, most progressive intellectuals and for that matter nationalist policy planners, middle-class citizens, journalists, and so on all over the world were also promoting watered-down versions of eugenic "science" in this era.) They shared in common with other versions of Darwinian thinking a new faith in social progress. Left-wing opinion thus had debts to eugenics and feminism but moved away from evolutionism's more repellently reactionary positions. Unlike Spencer, who believed that in the interests of social evolution the weak and deficient should be abandoned, Lu Hsun and his colleagues stood benevolently on the side of the weak. As they saw it power resided in the weakness of the oppressed, in women, in the peasant, in workers and in the child.

Starting in the late nineteenth century, and blossoming after the end of World War I, writing about women's liberation and about women's lives as social and theoretical terms, became ubiquitous in Chinese cities. Such writing included translated reports of women's position globally, social studies of gender relations, scientific reports on female physiology and gynecology, journalism about feminist progress in Turkey, Java, Japan, the United States, England, and Africa. Photojournalism exposed readers to racialised images of women. Although it is difficult to say for sure, it seems likely that male readers and writers drove this rage. That was not because women could not read or write. Female literacy in the elite social classes was relatively common, as the examples of Ding Ling and Yu Manzhen illustrate. Rather, high literacy among Chinese women tended to be rooted in conventions that were from the modernist perspective overly beholden to traditional aesthetics and poetics. On the other hand, newly professionalized, often bilingual in a European language or Japanese, the modern new men consumed broadsheets, newspapers, journals, magazines, and modernist books on the women question.

By the 1930s the question of women in Chinese feminism was an established part of semi-popular writing.

Questions of economic independence, political participation, birth control, heterosexuality as a norm, marriage and divorce, chastity, prostitution, female psychology and self-presentation, along with feminine ethics and sex education, were ways of classifying the women question for study and discussion. Even advertisements were endorsing modernist goals for female hygiene and personal choice. As occurred elsewhere, including the United States, one key question that emerged was the place of women's erotic desire and sexual expression in the good society. Gallons of ink were spilled in these debates, and the names of Freud, Darwin, Lester Ward, Maine, Westermark, Havelock Ellis, Margaret Sanger, and Ellen Key became familiar. So did Japanese contemporary theorists Kuriyakawa Hakuson (with Haeckel, one of Lu Hsun's favorites), Yosano Akiko, Yamakawa Kikue, and many lesser-known writers.

Educated Chinese opinion believed that female sexual self-expression would have a positive effect on progressive social development. Such opinion held, partly as an extension of eugenic thinking, that when women selected their own husbands they would in effect improve the Chinese race. Some arguments claimed that the female had originated life in primeval times and hence that sex selection, the basis of human evolution, should consequently be placed back into the hands of women. One exaggerated feminist position, for instance, held that, because Chinese had for centuries put sexual intercourse into the hands of parents, Chinese women were actually all prostitutes and their parents were all pimps.

This institutionalized prostitution system (also known as the Big Family system) had weakened the culture and led to its decline. Critics like this one echoed the truism that shortly became a bedrock modernist belief. Women can only be returned to humanity if they are allowed to choose their own way of life, including whom to have sex with, since each time a woman chooses she is unconsciously, selectively improving the overall racial quality of the Chinese people.

The stories we have chosen for this volume were part of these great debates about women's liberation. "New Years' Sacrifice," Lu Hsun's 1924 tale of murder by way of social convention, begins the volume. Xiang Lin Sao, according to this story, is blameless, pure, and stupid: she is as feral as the wolves who eat her son, and even more dim-witted than the respectable humans who torment her for ritual improprieties forced on her by others. Her tragedy is belief. She feeds her appetite for life with the good rice she earns in honest labor until quite literally she loses her appetite for life. Why? Xiang Lin Sao believes in the rubbish that passes for common sense in her claustrophobic provincial little world. In the dialectic of virtue and vice, she is virtuous and so witless from social disregard and derision that she believes the contemptible prejudices about ritual purity, sexual clan loyalty, the worship of sons, and the dispensability of women. The sacrifice of Sister Xiang to the conventions of the good old fashioned upright citizens, in utter disregard for her strong body and accommodating temperament, are a lesson in devolution. What if the rituals were abolished and the strong body and sweetness of the laboring woman celebrated? Surely the systematic cruelty the story catalogues would no longer be acceptable, and the society that promotes ignorance and pedantic self-righteousness would crumble. When a degenerate society eats its own strong and vulnerable people then it has no defenses against the global wolves, the "white peril" of the Great Powers, which in the 1920s were scouring the globe for more edible children. Lu Hsun's great story puts into the economical terms of a fiction the eugenic, geopolitical feminist critique of China's failures as a nation.

But notice how differently Ding Ling casts a similar story. Written in the heat of the revolutionary decampment to the Northwest and in the early days of the Second United Front against the Japanese imperialist army, the plot is not wholly different from Lu Hsun's piece. A weak member of the social group, a grandmother, is violated. Of course in this story the ravages of a culture gone bad, personified in "New Year Sacrifice" by the in-laws who sell Xiang Lin Sao and the second husband who rapes her, are replaced by rampaging enemy soldiers who rape and kill the community's girls and women. However, in a plot point redolent of Lu Hsun's earlier story, the ritual sexual violation of "chastity" or sexual loyalty to the patriline causes Grandma to lose her sense of propriety and babble about her experience. In part, of course the story illuminates the possibilitiy that, in a renovated society, tragedy can be recognized and trauma can be routed into social action. The Communist Party operatives arrive to mobilize the women into anti-Japanese war work and the promise of *fanshen*, of self-willed social revolutionary transformation. But the key difference in Ding Ling's story has to do with the way the victim appears to the reader.

The Grandma in "New Faith" has watched her grand-daughters raped and killed before her eyes. She was raped herself. In a village culture far more degraded by poverty, geographical isolation, unrelenting traditionalism, and war, than Lu Hsun's province town, rape is social death. But Grandma, famously, refuses to die. She survives the enemy and declines the social death those who love her would im-pose on her. Instead, and not always terribly lucidly, this aged, useless female victim talks. The metaphoric wolves of Lu Hsun's imagination have given way to real ones, and yet in the face of brutalization the female person in this story gets on with her life. She brushes aside the squeamishness of her sons and the chatter of villagers who would rather have seen ritual chastity upheld, and lives to tell a story of struggle and future triumph.

Reading Ding Ling's "Thoughts on March 8" and Lu Hsun's "What Happens after Nora Leaves Home?" together heightens the sense that, while the writers shared similar views of feminist ideas about progress and women's liberation, they disagreed fundamentally on who that creature in need of lib-eration was. It is hard to imagine disagreeing with Lu Hsun's point that slamming the door and blindly walking out of a family hell into the larger concerns of a society disinclined to accommodate free women is a brutal experience. Echo-ing the comments of theorists and militants alike, Lu Hsun's point is sociological. Until there is change, Nora and Zijun, protagonist of "Regret for the Past," will be the ultimate losers. They will give up the relative security of the patriarchy for the hostile unmooring of the premature revolutionary. But, just as she had disagreed with this position in her earliest writing, the famous collection *In Darkness*, Ding Ling's position, echoed in "Thoughts on March 8" is both less dramatic and in the end more optimistic. In the deceptively simple prose of the *zawen* genre she establishes at the outset that life for women, even in revolution, is tougher than life for men in the same revolution. That being said, however, there is also a social struggle going on and no woman can remain unarmed or unprotected since every woman will fight for justice and equality. Nora left home a long time ago. She survived social contempt, poverty, loneliness, self-inflicted wounds, and worse. Now at the center of the revolution and somewhat worse for the wear, this Nora is no silent shade or absent presence. With the violent sarcasm of the revolutionary purist, Ding Ling looks at Nora's afterlife from the perspective of the survivor.

One way to see how strongly the difference works is technical. Literature has its own technologies. In the short story form that Lu Hsun and Ding Ling each perfected, a narrator uniquely filters the unfolding action through a singular personality. For instance, the narrator of "Regret for the Past" (next of kin to the passive, alienated narrator from "New Year Sacrifice") opens his lament for his lover, Zijun, by usurping his lover's pain and replacing it with his own selfish remorse. How much do we ever learn about Zijun, since from beginning to end the fiction is filled with the narrator's account of his own feelings, his own obliviousness, his own petty cruelty, and his own torments. And of course in the famous conundrum of the representational order, Zijun cannot speak.

Compare Lu Hsun's bitterly cold technique of masculine self-loathing and feminine passivity to Ding Ling's masterpiece, "When I was in Xia Village." A middle-aged Communist cadre resolves to meet the woman who has caused a great uproar in an otherwise "civilized" and mobilized revolutionary peasant community behind the war front. The female narrator holds the position of authority. She has an escort, a reason for being placed in this village, and a recuperation of her own to make. When she takes the pulse of the villagers around her, as she seeks to discover why the arrival of a certain Zhenzhen from the front is causing consternation, the narrator seems scrupulously open and fair-minded. The narrative buildup to the meeting between the cadre and the girl can be seen almost sociologically as a survey of opinion. Even after they have met, the narrator is won over by the spirit of this brave girl who has returned to Xia village after a catastrophic rape and then, voluntarily working as a prostitute-spy behind the Japanese lines. Not only does this "Nora" figure speak, she is directly critical of prejudice and the disabling form of "love" that her fiancé and parents impose on her. Love cannot obscure the ruin that ritual violation of sexual purity imposes because, short of leaving for the Red capital of Yan'an, the only other course for Zhenzhen would be silence.

We note the hot singularity of Zhenzhen's character, of her passion despite the brutal way the world has treated her. The cool and observant narrator herself opens this world for readers to experience but, in distinction to Lu Hsun's claustrophobic chamber of horrors, this narrator is more like a colleague or coworker. She is on our side, the progressive side. Though the cruelties that she relays to us from the un-named villagers are conventional, the narrator is unflappably optimistic; there is much more the revolution will have to accomplish in this village, she indicates. And anyway the younger people are not as infected with the virus of the feu-dal society as their parents are. In fact the young speak to the cadre in admiring terms, noting Zhenzhen's fortitude and her courage. Everyone on the progressive side admits nonetheless that the world will have to change substantially before emancipation can find a socially safe place for the self-directed woman to live. Zhenzhen is in no danger of dying or becoming mute. Her life will be hard, but then so were all the alternatives.

I met Ding Ling in 1982. It was the end of my first year in the People's Republic. I got permission to travel to the seaside resort where she was staying. I still have grainy photographs of Ding Ling and me, and Ding Ling, her husband Chen Ming, and me. She was stout, and her bobbed hair was straight, gray, and thin. She dressed in the gray version of the simple clothes everyone wore in those days: thick cotton trousers, a lighter cotton blouse. When I think about her physical presence, however, I remember her sharp tongue and the aggressive posture of her body along with my shock at being so much taller than she. When we took a short walk along the beach, she reached into the surf and pulled out a stone-shaped piece of glass whitened from the friction of the surf, and gave it to me. I think it is somewhere among my belongings.

At first when I met her Ding Ling ridiculed me for asking so many questions about feminism and her work in the great feminist debates of the early forties. I remember that she told me to go home to my husband. But then, as we talked, and as I kept returning to visit her on a moment's notice, in between her interviews with important journalists and scholars, she warmed up to me. She bribed me with an offer to let me see rare photographs of herself, if only I would travel down south with her on the train. My time was running short, and I used that excuse to decline. But mostly I did not want to know so much about her life through the prism of her vengeance and suffering. How many years had she spent in prison dreaming of days like these. And I would be one more in the line of proxies for her revenge. She asked me to go to Stanford's Hoover library and find out if they had a genuine copy of GMD cadre Xu Enzeng's tattletale memoir of her years under his stewardship. I was to report back to her, which I did.

Tani E. Barlow
March 2007

NOTE

1. The publisher has chosen to retain the spelling of Lu Hsun, rather than Lu Xun, in order to remain in accordance with the spelling used in the original Foreign Language Press volumes, in which the translations of Lu Hsun's stories were originally published.

WORKS CITED

Alber, Charles. 2002. *Enduring the Revolution: Ding Ling and the Politics of Literature in Guomindang China*. New York: Praeger.

Barlow, Tani E. 2004. *The Question of Women in Chinese Feminism*. Durham: Duke University Press.

Denton, Kirk. 1998. Biography of Lu Hsun http://mclc.osu.edu/rc/bios/lxbio.htm.

Pusey, James Reeve. 1998. *Lu Xun and Evolution*. Albany: SUNY Press.

LU HSUN

THE NEW YEAR'S SACRIFICE

New Year's Eve of the old calendar[1] seems after all more like the real New Year's Eve; for, to say nothing of the villages and towns, even in the air there is a feeling that New Year is coming. From the pale, lowering evening clouds issue frequent flashes of lightning, followed by a rumbling sound of firecrackers celebrating the departure of the Hearth God; while, nearer by, the firecrackers explode even more violently, and before the deafening report dies away the air is filled with a faint smell of powder. It was on such a night that I returned to Luchen, my native place. Although I call it my native place, I had had no home there for some time, so I had to put up temporarily with a certain Mr. Lu, the fourth son of his family. He is a member of our clan, and belongs to the generation before mine, so I ought to call him "Fourth Uncle." An old student of the imperial college[2] who went in for Neo-Confucianism, I found him very little changed in any way, simply slightly older, but without any mustache as yet. When we met, after exchanging a few polite remarks he said I was fatter, and after saying that immediately started a violent attack on the revolutionaries. I knew this was not meant personally, because the object of the attack was still Kang Yuwei.[3] Nevertheless, conversation proved difficult, so that in a short time I found myself alone in the study.

The next day I got up very late, and after lunch went out to see some relatives and friends. The day after I did the same. None of them was greatly changed, simply slightly older; but every family was busy preparing for "the sacrifice." This is the great end-of-year ceremony in Luchen, when people reverently welcome the God of Fortune and solicit good fortune for the coming year. They kill chickens and geese and buy pork, scouring and scrubbing until all the women's arms turn red in the water. Some of them still wear twisted silver bracelets. After the meat is cooked some chopsticks are thrust into it at random, and this is called the "offering." It is set out at dawn when incense and candles are lit, and they reverently invite the God of Fortune to come and partake of the offering. Only men can be worshippers, and after the sacrifice they naturally continue to let off firecrackers as before. This happens every year, in every family, provided they can afford to buy the offering and firecrackers; and this year they naturally followed the old custom.

The day grew overcast. In the afternoon it actually started to snow, the biggest snow-flakes as large as plum blossom petals fluttered about the sky; and this, combined with the smoke and air of activity, made Luchen appear in a ferment.

When I returned to my uncle's study the roof of the house was already white with snow. The room also appeared brighter, the great red rubbing hanging on the wall showing up very clearly the character for Longevity written by the Taoist saint Chen Tuan.[4] One of a pair of scrolls had fallen down and was lying loosely rolled up on the long table, but the other was still hanging there, bearing the words: "By understanding reason we achieve tranquility of mind." Idly, I went to turn over the books on the table beneath the window, but all I could find was a pile of what looked like an incomplete set of *Kang Hsi's Dictionary*,[5] a volume of Chiang Yung's *Notes to Chu Hsi's Philosophical Writings* and a volume of *Commentaries on the Four Books*.[6] At all events, I made up my mind to leave the next day.

Besides, the very thought of my meeting with Hsiang Lin's Wife the day before made me uncomfortable. It happened in the afternoon. I had been visiting a friend in the eastern part of town. As I came out I met her by the river, and seeing the way she fastened her eyes on me I knew very well she meant to speak to me. Of all the people I had seen this time at Luchen none had changed as much as she: her hair, which had been streaked with white five years before, was now completely white, quite unlike someone in her forties. Her face was fearfully thin and dark in its sallowness, and had moreover lost its former expression of sadness, looking as if carved out of wood. Only an occasional flicker of her eyes showed she was still a living creature. In one hand she carried a wicker basket, in which was a broken bowl, empty;

in the other she held a bamboo pole longer than herself, split at the bottom: it was clear she had become a beggar.

I stood still, waiting for her to come and ask for money.

"You have come back?" she asked me first.

"Yes."

"That is very good. You are a scholar, and have traveled too and seen a lot. I just want to ask you something." Her lusterless eyes suddenly gleamed.

I never guessed she would talk to me like this. I stood there taken by surprise.

"It is this." She drew two paces nearer, and whispered very confidentially: "After a person dies, does he turn into a ghost or not?"

As she fixed her eyes on me I was seized with foreboding. A shiver ran down my spine and I felt more nervous than during an unexpected examination at school, when unfortunately the teacher stands by one's side. Personally, I had never given the least thought to the question of the existence of spirits. In this emergency how should I answer her? Hesitating for a moment, I reflected: "It is the tradition here to believe in spirits, yet she seems to be skeptical—perhaps it would be better to say she hopes: hopes that there is immortality and yet hopes that there is not. Why increase the sufferings of the wretched? To give her something to look forward to, it would be better to say there is."

"There may be, I think," I told her hesitantly.

"Then, there must also be a Hell?"

"What, Hell?" Greatly startled, I could only try to evade

the question. "Hell? According to reason there should be one too—but not necessarily. Who cares about it anyway? . . ."

"Then will all the people of one family who have died see each other again?"

"Well, as to whether they will see each other again or not. . . ." I realized now that I was a complete fool; for all my hesitation and reflection I had been unable to answer her three questions. Immediately I lost confidence and wanted to say the exact opposite of what I had previously said. "In this case . . . as a matter of fact, I am not sure. . . . Actually, regarding the question of ghosts, I am not sure either."

In order to avoid further importunate questions, I walked off, and beat a hasty retreat to my uncle's house, feeling exceedingly uncomfortable. I thought to myself: "I am afraid my answer will prove dangerous to her. Probably it is just that when other people are celebrating she feels lonely by herself, but could there be another reason? Could she have had some premonition? If there is another reason, and as a result something happens, then, through my answer, I shall be held responsible to a certain extent." Finally, however, I ended by laughing at myself, thinking that such a chance meeting could have no great significance, and yet I was taking it so to heart; no wonder certain educationalists called me a neurotic. Moreover I had distinctly said, "I am not sure," contradicting my previous answer; so that even if anything did happen, it would have nothing at all to do with me.

"I am not sure" is a most useful phrase.

Inexperienced and rash young men often take it upon themselves to solve people's problems for them or choose doctors for them, and if by any chance things turn out badly, they are probably held to blame; but by simply concluding with this phrase "I am not sure," one can free oneself of all responsibility. At this time I felt even more strongly the necessity for such a phrase, since even in speaking with a beggar woman there was no dispensing with it.

However, I continued to feel uncomfortable, and even after a night's rest my mind kept running on this, as if I had a premonition of some untoward development. In that oppressive snowy weather, in the gloomy study, this discomfort increased. It would be better to leave: I should go back to town the next day. The boiled shark's fins in the Fu Hsing Restaurant used to cost a dollar for a large portion, and I wondered if this cheap and delicious dish had increased in price or not. Although the friends who had accompanied me in the old days had scattered, even if I was alone the shark's fins still had to be tasted. At all events, I made up my mind to leave the next day.

After experiencing many times that things which I hoped would not happen and felt should not happen invariably did happen, I was desperately afraid this would prove another such case. And, indeed, strange things did begin to happen. Towards evening I heard talking—it sounded like a discussion—in the inner room; but soon the conversation ended, and all I heard was my uncle saying loudly as he walked out: "Not earlier nor later, but just at this time—sure sign of a bad character!"

At first I felt astonished, then very uncomfortable, thinking these words must refer to me. I looked outside the door, but no one was there. I contained myself with difficulty till their servant came in before dinner to brew a pot of tea, when at last I had a chance to make some enquiries.

"With whom was Mr. Lu angry just now?" I asked.

"Why, still with Hsiang Lin's Wife," he replied briefly.

"Hsiang Lin's Wife? How was that?" I asked again.

"She's dead."

"Dead?" My heart suddenly missed a beat. I started, and probably changed color too. But since he did not raise he head, he was probably quite unaware of how I felt. Then I controlled myself, and asked:

"When did she die?"

"When? Last night, or else today, I'm not sure."

"How did she die?"

"How did she die? Why, poverty of course." He answered placidly and, still without having raised his head to look at me, went out.

However, my agitation was only short-lived, for now that something I had felt imminent had already taken place, I no longer had to take refuge in my "I'm not sure," or the servant's expression "dying of poverty" for comfort. My heart already felt lighter. Only from time to time something still seemed to weigh on it. Dinner was served, and my uncle solemnly accompanied me. I wanted to ask about Hsiang

Lin's Wife, but knew that although he had read, "Ghosts and spirits are properties of Nature,"[7] he had retained many superstitions, and on the eve of this sacrifice it was out of the question to mention anything like death or illness. In case of necessity one could use veiled allusions, but unfortunately I did not know how to, so although questions kept rising to the tip of my tongue, I had to bite them back. From his solemn expression I suddenly suspected that he looked on me as choosing not earlier nor later but just this time to come and trouble him, and that I was also a bad character; therefore to set his mind at rest I told him at once that I intended to leave Luchen the next day and go back to the city. He did not press me greatly to stay. So we quietly finished the meal.

In winter the days are short and, now that it was snowing, darkness already enveloped the whole town. Everybody was busy beneath the lamplight, but outside the windows it was very quiet. Snow-flakes fell on the thickly piled snow, as if they were whispering, making me feel even more lonely. I sat by myself under the yellow gleam of the vegetable oil lamp and thought, "This poor woman, abandoned by people in the dust as a tiresome and worn-out toy, once left her own imprint in the dust, and those who enjoy life must have wondered at her for wishing to prolong her existence; but now at least she has been swept clear by eternity. Whether spirits exist or not I do not know; but in the present world when a meaningless existence ends, so that someone whom others are tired of seeing is no longer seen, it is just as well, both for the individual concerned and for others." I listened quietly to see if I could hear the snow falling outside the window, still pursuing this train of thought, until gradually I felt less ill at ease.

Fragments of her life, seen or heard before, now combined to form one whole.

She did not belong to Luchen. One year at the beginning of winter, when my uncle's family wanted to change their maidservant, Old Mrs. Wei brought her in and introduced her. Her hair was tied with white bands, she wore a black skirt, blue jacket and pale green bodice, and was about twenty-six, with a pale skin but rosy cheeks. Old Mrs. Wei called her Hsiang Lin's Wife, and said that she was a neighbor of her mother's family, and because her husband was dead she wanted to go out to work. My uncle knitted his brows and my aunt immediately understood that he disapproved of her because she was a widow. She looked very suitable, though, with big strong feet and hands, and a meek expression; and she had said nothing but showed every sign of being tractable and hard-working. So my aunt paid no attention to my uncle's frown, but kept her. During the period of probation she worked from morning till night, as if she found resting dull, and she was so strong that she could do a man's work; accordingly on the third day it was settled, and each month she was to be paid five hundred cash.

Everybody called her Hsiang Lin's Wife. They did not ask her her own name; but since she was introduced by someone from Wei Village who said she was a neighbor,

presumably her name was also Wei. She was not very talkative, only answering when other people spoke to her, and
her answers were brief. It was not until a dozen days or so
had passed that they learned little by little that she still had
a severe mother-in-law at home and a younger brother-in-
law more than ten years old, who would cut wood. Her
husband, who had been a woodcutter too, had died in the
spring. He had been ten years younger than she.[8] This little
was all that people learned from her.

The days passed quickly. She worked as hard as ever;
she would eat anything, and did not spare herself. Everybody
agreed that the Lu family had found a very good maidservant,
who really got through more work than a hard-working man.
At the end of the year she swept, mopped, killed chickens and
geese and sat up to boil the sacrificial meat, single-handed, so
the family did not have to hire extra help. Nevertheless she,
on her side, was satisfied; gradually the trace of a smile appeared at the corner of her mouth. She became plumper and
her skin whiter.

New Year was scarcely over when she came back from
washing rice by the river looking pale, and said that in the
distance she had just seen a man wandering on the opposite
bank who looked very like her husband's cousin, and probably he had come to look for her. My aunt, much alarmed,
made detailed enquiries, but failed to get any further information. As soon as my uncle learned of it he frowned
and said, "This is bad. She must have run away from her
husband's family."

Before long this inference that she had run away was confirmed.

About a fortnight later, just as everybody was beginning to forget what had happened, Old Mrs. Wei suddenly called, bringing with her a woman in her thirties who, she said, was the maidservant's mother-in-law. Although the woman looked like a villager, she behaved with great self-possession and had a ready tongue in her head. After the usual polite remarks she apologized for coming to take her daughter-in-law home, saying there was a great deal to be done at the beginning of spring, and since there were only old people and children at home they were short-handed.

"Since it is her mother-in-law who wants her to go back, what is there to be said?" was my uncle's comment.

Thereupon her wages were reckoned up. They amounted to one thousand seven hundred and fifty cash, all of which she had left with her mistress without using a single coin. My aunt gave the entire amount to her mother-in-law. The latter also took her clothes, thanked Mr. and Mrs. Lu and went out. By this time it was already noon.

"Oh, the rice! Didn't Hsiang Lin's Wife go to wash the rice?" my aunt exclaimed some time later. Probably she was rather hungry, so that she remembered lunch.

Thereupon everybody set about looking for the rice basket. My aunt went first to the kitchen, then to the hall, then to the bedroom; but not a trace of it was to be seen anywhere. My uncle went outside, but could not find it either; only when he went right down to the riverside did he see it, set down fair and square on the bank, with a bundle of vegetables beside it.

Some people there told him that a boat with a white awning had moored there in the morning, but since the awning covered the boat completely they did not know who was inside, and before this incident no one had paid any attention to it. But when Hsiang Lin's Wife came to wash rice, two men looking like country people jumped off the boat just as she was kneeling down and seizing hold of her carried her on board. After several shouts and cries, Hsiang Lin's Wife became silent: they had probably stopped her mouth. Then two women walked up, one of them a stranger and the other Old Mrs. Wei. When the people who told this story tried to peep into the boat they could not see very clearly, but Hsiang Lin's Wife seemed to be lying bound on the floor of the boat.

"Disgraceful! Still . . ." said my uncle.

That day my aunt cooked the midday meal herself, and my cousin Ah Niu lit the fire.

After lunch Old Mrs. Wei came again.

"Disgraceful!" said my uncle.

"What is the meaning of this? How dare you come here again!" My aunt, who was washing dishes, started scolding as soon as she saw her. "You recommended her yourself, and then plotted to have her carried off, causing all this stir. What will people think? Are you trying to make a laughingstock of our family?"

"Aiya, I was really taken in! Now I have come specifically to clear up this business. When she asked me to find her work, how was I to know that she had left home without her mother-in-law's consent? I am very sorry, Mr. Lu, Mrs. Lu. Because I am so old and foolish and careless, I have offended my patrons. However, it is lucky for me that your family is always so generous and kind, and unwilling to be hard on your inferiors. This time I promise to find you someone good to make up for my mistake."

"Still . . ." said my uncle.

Thereupon the business of Hsiang Lin's Wife was concluded, and before long it was also forgotten.

Only my aunt, because the maidservants taken on afterwards were all lazy or fond of stealing food, or else both lazy and fond of stealing food, with not a good one in the lot, still often spoke of Hsiang Lin's Wife. On such occasions she would always say to herself, "I wonder what has become of her now?" meaning that she would like to have her back. But by the following New Year she too gave up hope.

The New Year's holiday was nearly over when Old Mrs. Wei, already half tipsy, came to pay her respects, and said it was because she had been back to Wei Village to visit her mother's family and stayed a few days that she had come late. During the course of conversation they naturally came to speak of Hsiang Lin's Wife.

"She?" said Mrs. Wei cheerfully. "She is in luck now. When her mother-in-law dragged her home, she had already promised her to the sixth son of the Ho family in Ho Village. Not long after she reached home they put her in the bridal chair and sent her off."

"Aiya! What a mother-in-law!" exclaimed my aunt in amazement.

"Ah, madam, you really talk like a great lady! We country folk, poor women, think nothing of that. She still had a younger brother-in-law who had to be married. And if they hadn't found her a husband, where would they have found this money for his wedding?[9] But her mother-in-law is a clever and capable woman, who knows how to drive a good bargain, so she married her off into the mountains. If she had married her to someone in the same village, she wouldn't have got so much money; but since very few women are willing to marry someone living deep in the mountains, she got eighty thousand cash. Now the second son is married, the presents only cost her fifty thousand, and after paying the wedding expenses she still has over ten thousand left. Just think, doesn't this show she knows how to drive a good bargain? . . ."

"But was Hsiang Lin's Wife willing?"

"It wasn't a question of being willing or not. Of course anyone would have protested. They just tied her up with a rope, stuffed her into the bridal chair, carried her to the man's house, put on the bridal headdress, performed the ceremony in the hall and locked them in their room; and that was that. But Hsiang Lin's Wife is quite a character. I heard she really put up a great struggle, and everybody said she was different from the other people because she had worked in a scholar's family. We go-betweens, madam, see a great deal. When widows re-marry, some cry and shout, some threaten to commit suicide, some when they have been carried to the man's house won't go through the ceremony, and some even smash the wedding candlesticks. But Hsiang Lin's Wife was different from the rest. They said she shouted and cursed all the way, so that by the time they had carried her to Ho Village she was completely hoarse. When they dragged her out of the chair, although the two chair-bearers and her young brother-in-law used all their strength, they couldn't force her to go through the ceremony. The moment they were careless enough to loosen their grip—gracious Buddha!—she threw herself against a corner of the table and knocked a big hole in her head. The blood poured out; and although they used two handfuls of incense ashes and bandaged her with two pieces of red cloth, they still couldn't stop the bleeding. Finally it took all of them together to get her shut up with her husband in the bridal chamber, where she went on cursing. Oh, it was really dreadful!" She shook her head, cast down her eyes and said no more.

"And after that what happened next?" asked my aunt.

"They said the next day she still didn't get up," said Old Mrs. Wei, raising her eyes.

"And after?"

"After? She got up. At the end of the year she had a baby, a boy, who was two this New Year.[10] These few days when I was at home some people went to Ho Village, and when they came back they said they had seen her and her son, and that both mother and baby are fat. There is no mother-in-law over her, the man is a strong fellow who can earn a living, and the house is their own. Well, well, she is really in luck."

After this even my aunt gave up talking of Hsiang Lin's Wife.

But one autumn, two New Years after they heard how lucky Hsiang Lin's Wife had been, she actually reappeared on the threshold of my uncle's house. On the table she placed a round bulb-shaped basket, and under the eaves a small roll of bedding. Her hair was still wrapped in white bands, and she wore a black skirt, blue jacket and pale green bodice. But her skin was sallow and her cheeks had lots their color; she kept her eyes downcast, and her eyes, with their tear-stained rims, were no longer bright. Just as before, it was Old Mrs. Wei, looking very benevolent, who brought her in, and who explained at length to my aunt:

"It was really a bolt from the blue. Her husband was so strong, nobody could have guessed that a young fellow like that would die of typhoid fever. First he seemed better, but then he ate a bowl of cold rice and the sickness came back. Luckily she had the boy, and she can work, whether it is chopping wood, picking tea-leaves or raising silkworms; so at first she was able to carry on. Then who could believe that the child, too, would be carried off by a wolf? Although it was nearly the end of spring, still wolves came to the village—how could anyone have guessed that? Now she is all on her own. Her brother-in-law came to take the house, and turned her out; so she has really no way open to her but to come and ask help from her former mistress. Luckily this time there is nobody to stop her, and you happen to be wanting a new servant, so I have brought her here. I think someone who is used to your ways is much better than a new hand. . . ."

"I was really stupid, really . . ." Hsiang Lin's Wife raised her listless eyes to say. "I only knew that when it snows the wild beasts in the glen have nothing to eat and may come to the villages; I didn't know that in spring they came too. I got up at dawn and opened the door, filled a small basket with beans and called our Ah Mao to go and sit on the threshold and shell the beans. He was very obedient and always did as I told him: he went out. Then I chopped wood at the back of the house and washed the rice, and when the rice was in the pan and I wanted to boil the beans I called Ah Mao, but there was no answer; and when I went out to look, all I could see was beans scattered on the ground, but no Ah Mao. He never went to other families to play; and in fact at each place where I went to ask, there was no sign of him. I became desperate, and begged people to go look for him. Only in the afternoon, after looking everywhere else, did they go to look in the glen and see one of his little shoes caught on a bramble. 'That's bad,' they said, 'he must have met a wolf.' And sure enough when they went further in there he was, lying in the wolf's lair, with all his entrails eaten away, his hand still tightly clutching that little basket.

. . ." At this point she started crying, and was unable to complete the sentence.

My aunt had been undecided at first, but by the end of this story the rims of her eyes were rather red. After thinking for a moment she told her to take the round basket and bedding into the servants' quarters. Old Mrs. Wei heaved a long sigh as if relieved of a great burden. Hsiang Lin's Wife looked a little more at ease than when she first came and, without having to be told the way, quietly took away her bedding. From this time on she worked again as a maidservant in Luchen.

Everybody still called her Hsiang Lin's Wife.

However, she had changed a great deal. She had not been there more than three days before her master and mistress realized that she was not as quick as before. Since her memory was much worse, and her impassive face never showed the least trace of a smile, my aunt already expressed herself very far from satisfied. When the woman first arrived, although my uncle frowned as before, because they invariably had such difficulty in finding servants he did not object very strongly, only secretly warned my aunt that while such people may seem very pitiful they exert a bad moral influence. Thus although it would be all right for her to do ordinary work she must not join in the preparations for sacrifice; they would have to prepare all the dishes themselves, for otherwise they would be unclean and the ancestors would not accept them.

The most important event in my uncle's household was the ancestral sacrifice, and formerly this had been the busiest time for Hsiang Lin's Wife; but now she had very little to do. When the table was placed in the center of the hall and the curtain fastened, she still remembered how to set out the winecups and chopsticks in the old way.

"Hsiang Lin's Wife, put those down!" said my aunt hastily. "I'll do it!"

She sheepishly withdrew her hand and went to get the candlesticks.

"Hsiang Lin's Wife, put those down!" cried my aunt hastily again. "I'll fetch them."

After walking round several times without finding anything to do, Hsiang Lin's Wife could only go hesitantly away. All she did that day was to sit by the stove and feed the fire.

The people in the town still called her Hsiang Lin's Wife, but in a different tone from before; and although they talked to her still, their manner was colder. She did not mind this in the least, only, looking straight in front of her, she would tell everybody her story, which night or day was never out of her mind.

"I was really stupid, really," she would say. "I only knew when it snows the wild beasts in the glen have nothing to eat and may come to the villages; I didn't know that in spring they came too. I got up at dawn and opened the door, filled a small basket with beans and called our Ah Mao to go and sit on the threshold and shell them. He was very obedient and always did as I told him: he went out. Then I chopped wood at the back of the house and washed the rice, and when the rice was in the pan and I wanted to boil the beans I called Ah Mao, but there was no answer; and when I went out to look, all I could see was beans scattered on the ground, but no Ah Mao. He never went to other families to play; and in fact at each place where I went to ask, there was no sign of him. I became desperate, and begged people to go look for him. Only in the afternoon, after looking everywhere else, did they go to look in the glen and see on of his little shoes caught on a bramble. 'That's bad,' they said, 'he must have met a wolf.' And sure enough when they went further in there he was, lying in the wolf's lair, with all his entrails eaten away, his hand still tightly clutching that small basket. . . ." At this point she would start crying and her voice would trail away.

This story was rather effective, and when men heard it they often stopped smiling and walked away disconcerted, while the women not only seemed to forgive her but their faces immediately lost their contemptuous look and they added their tears to hers. There were some old women who had not heard her speaking in the street, who went specially to look for her, to hear her sad tale. When her voice trailed away and she started to cry, they joined in, shedding the tears which had gathered in their eyes. Then they sighed, and went away satisfied, exchanging comments.

She asked nothing better than to tell her sad story over and over again, often gathering three or four hearers. But before long everybody knew it by heart, until even in the eyes of the most kindly, Buddha fearing old ladies not a trace of tears could be seen. In the end, almost everyone in the town could recite her tale, and it bored and exasperated them to hear it.

"I was really stupid, really . . ." she would begin.

"Yes, you only knew that in snowy weather the wild beasts in the mountains had nothing to eat and might come down to the villages." Promptly cutting short her recital, they walked away.

She would stand there open-mouthed, looking at them with a dazed expression, and then go away too, as if she also felt disconcerted. But she still brooded over it, hoping from other topics such as small baskets, beans and other people's children, to lead up to the story of her Ah Mao. If she saw a child of two or three, she would say, "Oh dear, if my Ah Mao were still alive, he would be just as big. . . ."

Children seeing the look in her eyes would take fright and, clutching the hems of their mothers' clothes, try to tug them away. Thereupon she would be left by herself again, and finally walk away disconcerted. Later everybody knew what she was like, and it only needed a child present for them to ask her with an artificial smile, "Hsiang Lin's Wife, if your Ah Mao were alive, wouldn't he be just as big as that?"

She probably did not realize that her story, after having been turned over and tasted by people for so many days, had long since become stale, only exciting disgust and contempt; but from the way people smiled she seemed to know that they were cold and sarcastic, and that there was no need for her to say any more. She would simply look at them, not answering a word.

In Luchen people celebrate New Year in a big way: preparations start from the twentieth day of the twelfth month onwards. That year my uncle's household found it necessary to hire a temporary manservant, but since there was still a great deal to do they also called in another maidservant, Liu Ma, to help. Chickens and geese had to be killed; but Liu Ma was a devout woman who abstained from meat, did not kill living things, and would only wash the sacrificial dishes. Hsiang Lin's Wife had nothing to do but feed the fire. She sat there, resting, watching Liu Ma as she washed the sacrificial dishes. A light snow began to fall.

"Dear me, I was really stupid," began Hsiang Lin's Wife, as if to herself, looking at the sky and sighing.

"Hsiang Lin's Wife, there you go again," said Liu Ma, looking at her impatiently. "I ask you: that wound on your forehead, wasn't it then you got it?"

"Uh, huh," she answered vaguely.

"Let me ask you: what made you willing after all?"

"Me?"

"Yes. What I think is, you must have been willing; otherwise. . . ."

"Oh dear, you don't know how strong he was."

"I don't believe it. I don't believe he was so strong that you really couldn't keep him off. You must have been willing, only you put the blame on his being so strong."

"Oh dear, you . . . you try for yourself and see." She smiled.

Liu Ma's lined face broke into a smile too, making it

48

wrinkled like a walnut; her small beady eyes swept Hsiang Lin's Wife's forehead and fastened on her eyes. As if rather embarrassed, Hsiang Lin's Wife immediately stopped smiling, averted her eyes and looked at the snow-flakes.

"Hsiang Lin's Wife, that was really a bad bargain," continued Liu Ma mysteriously. "If you had held out longer or knocked yourself to death, it would have been better. As it is, after living with your second husband for less than two years, you are guilty of a great crime. Just think: when you go down to the lower world in future, these two men's ghosts will fight over you. To which will you go? The King of Hell will have no choice but to cut you in two and divide you between them. I think, really. . . ."

Then terror showed in her face. This was something she had never heard in the mountains.

"I think you had better take precautions beforehand. Go to the Tutelary God's Temple and buy a threshold to be your substitute so that thousands of people can walk over it and trample on it, in order to atone for your sins in this life and avoid torment after death."

At the time Hsiang Lin's Wife said nothing, but she must have taken this to heart, for the next morning when she got up there were dark circles beneath her eyes. After breakfast she went to the Tutelary God's Temple at the west end of the village, and asked to buy a threshold. The temple priests would not agree at first, and only when she shed tears did they give a grudging consent. The price was twelve thousand cash.

She had long since given up talking to people, because Ah Mao's story was received with such contempt; but news of her conversation with Liu Ma that day spread, and many people took a fresh interest in her and came again to tease her into talking. As for the subject, that had naturally changed to deal with the wound on her forehead.

"Hsiang Lin's Wife, I ask you: what made you willing after all that time?" one would cry.

"Oh, what a pity, to have had this knock for nothing," another looking at her scar would agree.

Probably she knew from their smiles and tone of voice that they were making fun of her, for she always looked steadily at them without saying a word, and finally did not even turn her head. All day long she kept her lips tightly closed, bearing on her head the scar which everyone considered a mark of shame, silently shopping, sweeping the floor, washing vegetables, preparing rice. Only after nearly a year did she take from my aunt her wages which had accumulated. She changed them for twelve silver dollars, and asking for leave went to the west end of the town. In less time than it takes for a meal she was back again, looking much comforted, and with an unaccustomed light in her eyes. She told my aunt happily that she had bought a threshold in the Tutelary God's Temple.

When the time came for the ancestral sacrifice at the winter equinox, she worked harder than ever, and seeing my aunt take out the sacrificial utensils and with Ah Niu carry the table into the middle of the hall, she went confidently to fetch the winecups and chopsticks.

"Put those down, Hsiang Lin's Wife!" my aunt called out hastily.

She withdrew her hand as if scorched, her face turned ashen-grey, and instead of fetching the candlesticks she just stood there dazed. Only when my uncle came to burn incense and told her to go, did she walk away. This time the change in her was very great, for the next day not only were her eyes sunken, but even her spirit seemed broken. Moreover she became very timid, not only afraid of the dark and shadows, but also of the sight of anyone. Even her own master or mistress made her look as frightened as a little mouse that has come out of its hold in the daytime. For the rest, she would sit stupidly, like a wooden statue. In less than half a year her hair began to turn grey, and her memory became much worse, reaching a point when she was constantly forgetting to go and prepare the rice.

"What has come over Hsiang Lin's Wife? It would really have been better not to have kept her that time." My aunt would sometimes speak like this in front of her, as if to warn her.

However, she remained this way, so that it was impossible to see any hope of her improving. They finally decided to get rid of her and tell her to go back to Old Mrs. Wei. While I was at Luchen they were still only talking of this; but judging by what happened later, it is evident this is what they must have done. Whether after leaving my uncle's household she became a beggar, or whether she went first to Old Mrs. Wei's house and later became a beggar, I do not know.

. . .

I was woken up by firecrackers exploding noisily close at hand, saw the glow of the yellow oil lamp as large as a bean, and heard the splutter of fireworks as my uncle's household celebrated the sacrifice. I knew that it was nearly dawn. I felt bewildered, hearing as in a dream the confused continuous sound of distant crackers which seemed to form one dense cloud of noise in the sky, joining the whirling snow-flakes to envelop the whole town. Wrapped in this medley of sound, relaxed and at ease, the doubt which had preyed on me from dawn to early night was swept clean away by the atmosphere of celebration, and I felt only that the saints of heaven and earth had accepted the sacrifice and incense and were all reeling with intoxication in the sky, preparing to give the people of Luchen boundless good fortune.

February 7, 1924

NOTES

1. The Chinese lunar calendar.

2. The highest institute of learning in the Ching dynasty.

3. A famous reformist who lived from 1858 to 1927 and advocated constitutional monarchy.

4. A hermit at the beginning of the tenth century.

5. A Chinese dictionary compiled under the auspices of Emperor Kang Hsi who reigned from 1662 to 1722.

6. Confucian classics.

7. A Confucian saying. The Confucians took a relatively rational view of spirits.

8. In old China it used to be common in country districts for young women to be married to boys of ten or eleven. The bride's labor could then be exploited by her husband's family.

9. In old China, because of the labor value of the peasant woman, the man's family virtually bought the wife.

10. It was the custom in China to reckon a child as one year old at birth, and to add another year to his age at New Year.

DING LING

NEW FAITH

—

I

Beyond the meager stands of trees, on the farthest reach of the plain, the village of Xiliu lay serenely.[1] Leafless branches of the willows along the embankment outside the village whipped madly in the blasting winter wind. Under the willow trees, a whitewashed, mud-brick wall glimmered in the frozen slush, the sickly ashen white augmenting the bitter, forbidding gloom. A tall pagodalike building stood alone at the village gate. It looked like a lonely old man, wrapped in black garments sheened with age, standing at dusk gazing forlornly into the distance.

It really was dusk. The village rested in an evening haze. Yet virtually none of the mist came from dinner fires.

One after another, flocks of crows circled above the village, then flew off to the jujube grove on the hillside. Little birds that had already found their roosts in the grove chirped uncertainly, startled by the new arrivals.

What really alarmed them was the looming shadow of a man walking heavily down the hillside. At each step, his old, black, wadded-cotton shoes made a crunching noise as they shattered the thin layer of ice frozen on the tufts of grass. A wild hen with beautiful plumage fled in fear toward the grove.

Like a prisoner on his way to execution, Chen Xinhan used all his strength to keep from falling down. His listless eyes stared blankly at the sky; seemingly terrified that he might catch sight of something horrible, he hardly dared glance around. His footsteps slowed still further as he rounded the bottom of the hill.

The village was no longer deadly silent, but, like a patient just waking from a coma, moaned tiredly. It was already dark. What was that tapping noise? It sounded like a hoe striking the frozen ground. He couldn't tell from the women's voices whether they were calling or sobbing, so much did they sound like choruses of doleful, starving wolves howling late at night on the empty mountaintop. Urgent, wincing terror gripped Chen Xinhan as he heard these sounds clear as a bell. He couldn't stop a shudder from running through his body. He stood stupefied. Then, mustering courage once again, and drawn by desperate hope, he walked down the hill toward a village now encompassed in an iridescent midst that left only the vague outlines of rooftops visible.

Two human shapes moved out of the village through the evening darkness, soundlessly, single file, carrying something. When Chen Xinhan realized that the object they were carrying between them was a human body, he felt stricken. His steps became increasingly hesitant. He felt a rekindled anxiety. He walked to a spot close by and watched them, carefully noting every move they made.

Digging fitfully into the earth beside the body, the two men soon rapidly, vigorously tossed loose soil back into the pit, gradually filling it up. Then they packed it down, leaving a raised earthen mound in the shape of a *mantou* bun.[2] After a few final pats, the two men turned back to the familiar path and headed for home. By mutual consent not a word had been spoken. Only as they left did one of the two sigh deeply.

"Hey, hey, tell me. Who's in that hole? Who is it?" Chen Xinhan grabbed at them. The moaning timbre of a sick animal sounded in his voice.

"It's Mister Zhang.[3] We found him in his grandson's house. He'd probably been dumped there," one of them answered.

"His granddaughter-in-law was lying stark naked right next to him," the other continued. "She was stuck to the ground by her own congealed blood. Look. She's right over there sleeping so peacefully now. The one on the right."

Chen Xinhan let them go and fell in behind them. There was something lodged in his throat that he dared not say aloud. The younger of the two men broke the silence: "Where'd you run off to the last couple of days, Uncle Chen.[4] Better get on home fast. Your brother's already back."

"Erguan?[5] When did he get back?" Chen didn't wait

for the answer. His legs had found new strength, his stride lengthened; he raised his head as one scene after another ran through his mind. Though trivial, these incidents still moved him deeply.

By then they'd entered the village proper. The darkness made it impossible to tell if any major changes had occurred, so his fearfulness changed to hope. Chen Xinhan left the gravediggers behind. He rushed off toward his house.

He'd left it five days before. Around dawn he'd heard a burst of gunfire coming from just outside the village. He'd leaped out of bed. His wife was already up, and his fifteen-year-old daughter, Jingu, ashen faced, came bursting into the room.[6] Everybody knew what was happening. "Run!" he said. "Get to Granny's house by the back route on the other side of the hill."[7]

"Daddy, oh, Daddy! If we have to die, let's die together."

"Where's my sheepskin vest?"

"Don't worry about your things now! The Japs are nearly here . . ."

He'd dragged out his bound-foot wife with one hand, his pretty young daughter with the other. Jingu ran crazed with panic. Her face looked hideous, disguised with smears of soot and dirt. They ran ahead of the crowd and soon reached the top of the hill. But then his wife started sobbing. Had their second daughter and their son gotten away? And what about Chen Xinhan's fifty-seven-year-old mother? So leaving the women to flee with the crowd, he slipped off and went back toward the village. People grabbed him, saying, "Don't turn back! Run for your life!" but he didn't know the meaning of fear because his only concern was to rescue his mother. He searched the sweeping tide of people shouting her name.

His sister-in-law, Erguan's wife, limped up to him, lugging her one-year-old daughter.

"Mama? Have you seen Mama?"

"A little while ago. She got out before me. She's got Yingu and Tongguan. Where're we going?"

"Granny's. Hurry!"

But he couldn't flee with her. Instead he headed for home. The village was in total chaos. Bullets flew around his head, people screamed for help. The outlying houses were in flames, and white smoke rolled into the village. There wasn't a soul at his house, just a few chickens darting around the courtyard screeching. He nearly walked right into a hail of bullets. With a shout, he dodged back. He could hear hoofbeats bearing down on him but couldn't risk the time to glance at his rear. The skies were falling, the earth splitting behind him. Crushed, people hadn't the time to draw their next breath; only the sounds of a sharp cry, gasps.

Nor did he find any of his family along the road back. He traded inquiries with several people from the village he came across, but nobody could give any satisfactory answers.

He walked over to look at two old crones sitting at the top of the hill whining and sobbing with grief, but neither of them was his mother. Exhausted children straggled along, none of them his Tongguan. And now he couldn't even find his wife and daughter. If only he could find Erguan's wife, everything would be fine. But not a trace of her was to be seen. He rested and waited around a bit, as refugees streamed past, yet not one of them was a member of his family.

"It was a whole regiment!"

"They hacked farmhands to death!"

"Will our Xiliu Village be destroyed this time?"

"I kept telling you they'd come!"

"So now we're all going to get it."

"This . . . This was preordained."

Panic was more contagious standing there in a crowd, so he went off by himself. He walked to the village of Zhangjiawan, about twelve miles away. Only twenty or thirty families lived there. It had always been a very quiet place without much coming and going, and the people there had few connections with outsiders. Their existence resembled that of primitive people. His wife's parents lived there.

No one else came that evening after he arrived to join his wife and Jingu. He spent the whole next day searching and hearing nothing but bad news about the village. On the third day, he sent word to his brothers. On the fourth, he got a return message. They reported that they'd be going home before long—beyond that nothing was certain. On the fifth day, he went out again and had good news by afternoon. The guerrillas had retaken Xiliu, and people had already begun moving back. So he did too, just to see how things stood. He was very frightened. He couldn't bear thinking about what might have happened to his family there, but he had to go back. Harried and anxious, he had left for home.

Now he was already feeling better. He'd seen nothing unpropitious, perhaps because nothing bad had happened. The two gravediggers, however, had neglected to tell him one thing: that very afternoon they'd buried a boy named Tongguan. His only son.

II

"Let me go with you guys to get it." Jingu tightened her belt and looked up at her Second Uncle, Chen Zuohan, ignoring her mother's venomous gaze.

The second son after Chen Xinhan, Chen Zuohan had inherited their father's character, his boldness and his sobriety. Whenever Chen Zuohan scowled or pursed his lips, the other brothers would exchange glances and keep quiet, and his mother would shrink quietly away to the kitchen or next room to eavesdrop. But he didn't get angry often, and was much too indulgent with the children, which always made the women grumpy.

"Better not come. Stay home. Besides, it's still snowing outside." He patted her thinly padded jacket.

"No. I want to go." Jingu turned around, pouting. "I don't want to sit around inside." She rolled her eyes, looked over at her mother and aunt, then turned back, letting her beseeching gaze stop on the face of her uncle.

Her uncle smiled as though to say, "What a child."

"Shameless bitch!" Her mother's temper had turned

perverse and difficult recently. "A big girl like you," her abuse continued, "daring to go outside with all these soldiers on the rampage."

"Stay with you mother," Chen Xinhan said without looking at his daughter. He turned and went out.

"Jingu, get a fire started. Boil some water. Remember Second Uncle Zuohan might find Granny and Little Sissy. Now what are you after?" Jingu didn't answer. She covered her head with a cloth and started out the door. "Where are you going?" her mother asked sharply.

"I'm going out for coal, if that's all right with you," Jingu yelled back at her.

Uncle Zuohan grinned again. Then he glanced contemptuously around the room and went solemnly out the door.

Chen Xinhan's wife squatted at the head of the *kang* desperately racking her brains to find some way of venting her rage, someone to blame, when a new idea came to her all of a sudden. She was sure her insight was correct. Newly kindled rage gnawed at her guts. She felt a tremendous urge to bite into human flesh. Then she checked herself with effort.

"Second Sister-in-law," she said softly, "didn't you say you saw Granny with Tongguan and Yingu the day you escaped from the Japs?"

Second Sister-in-law, holding her baby and squatting at the other end of the *kang*, had grown frightened of her sister-in-law and was choosing her words carefully these last few days.

"Sure," she replied affably. "I saw them just as I was leaving."

"And when did you run into Jingu's dad?"

"Halfway down."

"Oh!"

Conversation stopped for a moment, and then she asked, "Had you ever been to Seventh Uncle's place before?"

"Never. I was running away with lots of other people. I don't know exactly how I got there. If he hadn't been out looking around, well . . . !" Second Sister-in-law recalled that terrible confusion. If she hadn't run into Seventh Uncle, what would have happened to her then?

"Well, now. Isn't that just a little too lucky to be true! I say, Second Sister-in-law, we're related, so you don't have to mince words with me. Jingu's father took you and the baby up there. Nothing wrong with that . . . I guess. . . . So why do you two think you can put one over on me?"

"Elder Sister-in-law! Don't be absurd! The whole family is in big, big trouble. Come on. Come on, cool down."

"Sure the family's in trouble, but none of it ever fell on your head. Didn't you and your son have someone to take you to a safe place? You should pity me. Ah, my Tongguan, my son. You died so hard!" Her fist pounded the *kang*, her tears flowed, and the resentment choking her coursed out like water, yet found itself magically replenished. Her teeth gnashed and she went on cursing, "They're all bastards here. Not one of them has any sympathy or sense of shame . . ." She kept searching for words that would humiliate Second

Sister-in-law, hoping she could get her angry.

Second Sister-in-law felt unfairly abused and wept under the quilt. Then, startled, the baby started shrieking.

"Ma, what's the matter? What's going on?" The scene baffled Jingu, on her way back in with a sack of coal.

The sound of her daughter's voice broke Chen Xin-han's wife's heart. Now she only had one daughter, and her younger girl had been so much cuter than this Jingu, so lively and obedient, and she'd never defied her mother. And she hadn't even seen Tongguan's corpse, only visited his little grave twice. She could imagine what he must have looked like. He'd been . . . he'd probably looked like a slaughtered lamb, with green, red, and white stuff oozing out of his slit-open belly. Every time she though about it, she wanted to vomit; she felt the same sort of unbearable pain she'd have had if her own guts had been ripped out.

"Ma! Don't cry! Second Auntie, you . . . what're you doing?" But then Jingu herself couldn't help bursting into sobs as well.

Nightfall brought snowfall, and the darkness pressed down on the snow. Thick, interminable, nebulous layers of clouds wafted slowly to the ground. The wind tore madly at the paper windows and poured in through the cracks. Inside twilight turned to darkness. People's feelings changed too, from anxious resentment to deep grief. Their sobbing subsided. They groaned as they mourned the dead.

Second Sister-in-law gingerly put the baby, who'd fallen asleep from exhaustion, down on the *kang* and groped her way around the room; she didn't want to give anyone a reason to make trouble.

Jingu felt better once someone was moving around. The flames glowed in the stove and the air above the *kang* got warmer. Steam rising out of the boiling wok obscured the forms of those seated around the stove. They chatted again, exchanging their dreams. They began to wait in hope for their pitiful white-haired granny and innocent young daughter.

III

The North wind, swirling the silent snow, swept mercilessly across the plains and the hills on a rampage. Excruciating, bitter cold and the ravening darkness ruled the universe of night. Walls and roofs were scarce in this land laid waste. People huddled together like dogs. And the dogs curled up in the ruins, tails between their legs, so worn down that even when they saw something move, they'd just close their eyes again.

Chen Xinhan's family had spent most of the night in a fervor of hope. Now only Jingu was still on her feet, feeding the fire, adding more water to the steaming wok. Again and again she asked, "Second Uncle, do you think Granny will come back?"

"No, no. Not on a night this cold. Even if they found her, Third Uncle wouldn't let her come now." Chen Zuohan reclined on the *kang* smoking. "Go to sleep, child."

"Not unless you do. Look how soundly Mommy's sleeping."

"Mmm. The ordeal's worn her out."

Jingu, however, ignored his sympathetic remark. She questioned him on and on about what was going on in the village. She also talked to him about her grandmother. They both hoped she wouldn't come back that night because it was so cold.

Then they thought they could hear cries and moans mingled with the howling of the wind. Jingu was frozen with terror, looking at her uncle and holding up her hands as if to say, don't move! Listen! Her uncle held his breath and listened closely, for nothing could be seen in the darkness outside. Even her father, half asleep on the *kang*, sat up. But there was nothing there. Still they waited in the dim lamp-light until the sky turned as gray as a fish's belly and they were certain that their hopes would have to be postponed for another day. Soon it was just as silent inside as out.

A bleak day dawned. The endless blackness turned slowly to pale gray, and from the remote sky snowflakes came raining down thick and fast, whirling every downward. No birds sang. No cocks crowed. Even the dogs did not bark. The snow covered the destruction, the tattered mess; frozen, the ordure, animal bones, and feathers all became invisible. The entire blood-soaked land disappeared under the frozen snow. The only things left were black words on a white wall: "Extirpate Communism! Support the Greater East Asia Co-Prosperity Sphere!" written over the scrubbed out, faded inscription "Drive Japanese Imperialism out of China!" Now the darker words were being disfigured too, by rivulets of melting snow running like snot and tears down a weeping face.

There was only one living thing moving about on the plain. Then it too collapsed. Covered with snow, had it not begun instinctively to crawl forward again, it would have been impossible to spot. Gradually this living thing moved into the village. It was human. But no one was around in the village, and so the figure fell on the roadside again. It struggled up once more to drive off a curious dog. Weakly it waved its arms, tried to straighten its bent back. Fearfully, listing, it staggered toward a familiar house. The dog no longer recognized this human being. Listless, yet unwilling to leave it, the dog tailed it. A simple desire had brought the thing to Chen Xinhan's yard, but once there it lay immobile, like a broken tile, on the ground. Two greedy yellow eyes gazed down; it was too weak to drive the dog away again, too weak even to cry out. It could only moan and close its dry and withered eyes. Another dog came through a hole in the courtyard wall and barked twice. The first dog leaped forward, barking back. The body on the ground groaned again.

"Father!" cried newly awakened Jingu. "I hear something outside!"

"Dogfight."

"I hate that disgusting noise. I'll go chase them off."

Jingu slipped off the *kang* and picked up a lump of coal. Both dogs barked menacingly at her as she stepped through the doorway. She threw the coal at them and they ran off barking.

"She can't even leave the dogs alone," grumbled her mother under the quilt.

"Second Uncle! Hey, there's something in the yard!"

The girl stepped closer as the dogs barked furiously. Jingu drove them off then kicked at the body. It opened its eyes a little and moaned. Then Jingu uttered a horrified, inhuman shriek like a bamboo rent in two.

Following a lot of frantic activity, the body, now dressed in dry cotton-padded garments, lay unconscious on the warm *kang*. Strands of wispy hair glued onto the sockets of her empty, sunken eyes. Second Sister-in-law fed her hot rice gruel. Jingu threw herself down next to her mommy's feet and wept. The baby, who didn't recognize the granny who'd always carried him around and kissed him all the time, sat in a corner of the *kang* afraid to make a sound. Chen Xinhan had already gone for a doctor. His wife was sobbing uncontrollably as she though of her vanished daughter. She wanted her back!

"Ma, do you recognize us now?" Chen Zuohan asked repeatedly. But the old woman could not give him a satisfactory answer. She couldn't even gesture to him.

He watched her protectively, her terribly aged face, two dead, fishlike eyes inlaid in a piece of burnt wood. His hatred fanned into a great flame. "Ma." He directed each deliberate syllable toward that wooden face. "Ma! You can die in peace now. Your son will give his life to revenge you. I live on now only for Jap blood! I'll give my life for you, this village, Shanxi Province, the nation of China! I want Japanese blood so I can cleanse and fertilize our land. I want Jap blood!"

Like the intoned chant at an exorcism, his spell brought her slowly back to life. The old woman on the *kang* moved. Her lips quivered. "Japs!" she cried a moment later in mortal terror. She'd recovered consciousness. She looked speechlessly at her daughters-in-law and grandchildren, as tears streamed from her eyes; then, like a duck with its throat cut, wings flapping convulsively, neck writhing, she bent her head down and sobbed like a child.

"Granny! Granny! Granny!" The room was suffused with sorrow, to be sure. Yet new buds of warmth and hope had also begun to flower.

IV

The strength of her desire to live quickly restored the old woman's health. A few days later she was sitting in the yard sunning herself, surrounded by the other women in the family. She was telling a story.

"Oh, that girl screamed and yelled, pounded her legs like the sticks on a big drum, her pale white belly writhing . . ."

"Don't, Granny, don't. I'm scared!" Jingu hid her face in her hands.

"Three Japs climbed on her at the same time." She seemed to enjoy intimidating her granddaughter. "She couldn't even scream anymore; her face turned purple. . . . Unh . . . unh . . . unh . . . she moaned like a cow. Even childbirth isn't as painful as that. She looked at me, so I told her, 'Bite your tongue off. Bite! Hard!' I figured she'd be better off dead."

"Oh, Granny, Granny!" The women's faces blanched.

"She died too. But not from biting off her tongue," the old woman continued smugly. "Her naked carcass lay in a big pool of blood; more than if she'd had a baby. Her chest was all bloody too, blood running down her midriff, down her shoulders. They'd chewed off her little nipples." With demonic eyes she stared like a witch at her granddaughter's face. "Nipples no bigger than yours! Her sweet little face was all chewed up as well, like a maggoty apple. And she still kept looking at me with those big round eyes."

The old lady had changed. Didn't she love her own family anymore? Why was she always terrorizing them? When they sighed or cried, she'd become incensed and shout, "Go right ahead, cry your eyes out! Nothing but a pot of worthless piss. Just wait. The Japs will be back . . ." And if she saw their faces blaze red with anger, she'd feel quite satisfied at the fire she'd started.

At first she'd stop telling her stories when she saw her sons. She was afraid of their searching glances, and besides, the personal shame and sorrow she felt kept her from going on when they were around. She described how her other granddaughter had died. The thirteen-year-old child had served as a "comfort girl." Half dead of terror from being crushed under the heavy soldiers' bodies, she kept screaming for her mommy and grandma. She only "comforted" two soldiers before they threw her into a corner. She lived a day longer, tears visible on her ashen face. Just before the old lady was sent to the "Home of Respect for the Aged," they dragged Yingu off, still alive.[8] Her grandmother said that they probably threw her to the dogs alive.

She'd also witnessed Tongguan's death. She described it in detail without a thought to the unbearable grief it would cause her daughter-in-law. She said Tongguan was a good child because he wouldn't obey them. He kept on even with a bayonet pointed at him; when he tried to get away, the Jap skewered him and even then he didn't cry. He died well.

She'd seen too much. In the last ten days, she'd seen more evil than she'd witnessed before in her whole life. When the neighbors came to ask about their relatives she would tell them truthfully how their parents, wives, and children had been sacrificed under the butcher's knife and how, while alive, they had suffered endless pain.

The old lady had never been much of a talker, but now, seeing the effect her stories had, she felt a lot more comfortable. She got sympathy and understanding from telling stories, and it made her realize that other people shared the hatred she felt. For that reason, she just forgot to be timid. At first she tended to stutter and hesitate, and then she'd cry. But by watching her listeners' faces, she'd learned how to phrase her tales most effectively.

She told them about her own humiliations too, about what she'd had to do at the "Home." She'd washed their clothes, stitched their little Japanese flags, endured their whippings. Whenever she reached that point, she'd pull back her sleeves and unbutton her collar to show where her scars were. She'd also had to sleep with a man. An old Chinese man had been forced to do it to her while the Japs all stood around watching. "Please don't hate me," the old man had sobbed, as his tears fell on her face.

She began touring the entire village, crowds following behind her, pointing out all the places where specific atrocities had taken place.

"You're not going to forget this now, are you?" she'd shout at them belligerently.

Soon she was doing this every day, and if there was only a handful of people out in the street, she'd burst into somebody's house and, gesticulating wildly, harangue them there. Her listeners invariably forgot what they were supposed to be doing and, caught up by her emotions, would begin talking. The whole village knew her, particularly the children, who called on her frequently.

Her sons and daughters-in-law talked the situation over. "We've got a maniac in the family!" The eldest daughter-in-law was always the first to speak up. "Why, she isn't eating, and doesn't take care of her hair. Now she just won't stay home!"

"Granny sure has changed. When she talks about Tong-guan and Yingu, she doesn't shed a single tear. I really don't understand what's going on in her mind." The second daughter-in-law peeked at her husband. Lost in thought, he only frowned.

Chen Xinhan was thinking about the day before, when he'd gone over to listen to the old woman as she preached her stories in front of a crowd. When she got to the parts about what had happened to her personally, Xinhan had felt as though he were the one losing his mind. A son's blood coursed through his body, yet he didn't know whether to shout or go over and hug his mother or just run away. He shuddered violently, speechless all of a sudden, just as his mother caught sight of him and stopped telling her story to stare at him numbly. The audience turned around, but nobody laughed. He felt more misery than he'd ever experienced before. He walked over to her, put out his hand, and said, "I promise I'll get revenge!" Her face split with joy and she reached toward him as well, then suddenly shrank away. She shriveled up like a cornered animal, slipped through the crowd, and ran away. No one spoke. Heads bowed as though heavily weighted, people in the crowd moved away slowly, with dragging steps. He alone remained in the deserted street. He felt empty and, at the same time, as though he were being choked.

"The way I see it," Eldest Daughter-in-law started up again angrily, "the whole family's gone crazy. Why don't you say something to her? All this going on, and you act as if you're above it all."

"Say something? What do you want me to say? I know what she's suffering."

"So who isn't suffering?"

Chen Xinhan did not want to prolong this conversation. He did not want to quarrel with his mother just for the sake of argument. He looked at his brother.

His brother agreed with him. He asked the women if he

should get a rope and tie the old lady up to keep her from going out. He said he thought that everything would be all right so long as Jingu went along to keep an eye on her and stop her from offending anybody.

V

When her third son, Chen Lihan—her youngest and best loved—got back, he stroked his mother's white hair and stammered, "I apologize, Ma. You wouldn't have fallen into Jap hands if I'd been home that day. But you can't always have things your own way once you join the army."

"And what good would you be to me if you hadn't enlisted?" She looked her son over. He was a young man of twenty or so, wearing a short jacket, a pistol strapped to his waist. The sight of him seemed to satisfy her. "It's a world of guns now, Sanguan. Just tell me, how many Japs have you killed?"

She didn't need to complain to him about how she'd suffered, because he didn't need to be told. She vastly preferred listening to stories about fighting the Japanese, feeling more comfort from that.

"Well," her son said, "since you are not afraid of hearing about such things, I'll tell you."

Chen Lihan's face lit up immediately. He stood straight and tall and launched into his story: how they'd counterattacked and occupied this village, Xiliu, killing more than twenty Japs, and then moved on to retake Dongliu Village and Li Village; how they'd breached the Jap line at Sanyang Village, had had to retreat, but now held it once again. It

73

was impossible to remember for sure how many Japs they'd killed. They had captured a lot of war materiel, including rifles, bullets, and rations. He went on to say that among his group of men was the famous hero Zhang Dachuan, who'd gone to town on his own, with a light machine gun hidden under his jacket. There were too many Jap soldiers around, so he didn't use it there. But later, on his way out of town, he'd run into a dozen of the bastards, all just begging to die; so he'd shot the hell out of them. Chen Lihan also told about the time they'd caught a Jap soldier and how he and a bunch of the locals were carrying him between them on a pole. But this Jap was really fat. Somehow he'd gotten away from them along the way, and even with half a dozen of them trailing him, they never did get him back.

The old lady stuffed herself full of these stories and couldn't wait to find someone to retell them to. She'd gotten even more uninhibited lately because her oldest son, a member of the farmer's co-op, was off buying seed for the spring planting. Her second son had been drafted, and her third was gone four nights out of five. Besides, she wasn't in the least bit afraid of her third son. So one night when she saw two big trucks parked in the courtyard, she asked Chen Lihan, "Are they our trucks?"

"Yeah, they're ours. They're our transport trucks."

"Well, I don't care what they haul, even if it's pigs or dogs. So long as they're ours, I know what I'm going to do with them. Tomorrow I'm going to Wangjia Village."

They all turned and stared at her.

"What do you mean there's no room on them, that they're for hauling food?" She cut their objections short. "I don't care, I'm going. I want to see my brother and sister-in-law."

So the next day, she and Jingu rode a grain transport truck to Wangjia Village. She found her brother and his wife and told them all about the atrocities. Again she watched the falling tears, the belligerence that listening to her stories evoked in people. Then to soothe their wounded spirits, she acted out all the exciting, hortatory stories she'd just heard from her son, adding her own flourishes and making people smile again. She used the moment to urge everyone there to join the guerillas.

"You cowards!" she bawled, seeing them hesitate. "Afraid to die! Well, just wait 'til the Japs get here and butcher you all. I've seen them wipe out lots of powder puffs, just like you!"

Actually, many who heard her stories did join the guerrillas. Sometimes she'd lead a small group back home and hand them over to her son. "Take them," she'd say. "They all want to be like you. They all want guns."

After getting back from Wangjia, it was even harder for her to sit quietly at home, or even, for that matter, in Xiliu Village. So, taking Jingu along with her, she went to other villages. When there was no ride handy, she walked. "Why don't you talk too," she'd shout at Jingu.

Jingu was among the first to stand up for her grandma. She loved her and basked in the daily devotion she got from her. Each time Granny hustled her off on another trip, Jingu would gaze at her raptly in total understanding. Then Granny would embrace her, hugging her tightly, and heave a sigh of relief. It made Jingu feel warm inside again, but it was a happiness mixed with pain. Truth be told, Jingu was her grandmother's biggest supporter. Any time she talked privately with people, she'd use, with some embarrassment, phrases she'd picked up from her grandmother.

The love the old woman felt for her sons had also altered. Earlier, a great deal earlier, actually, she had thought of them as obedient little kittens. Later on, she'd only been concerned that they hurry up and grow into adults. She longed for the time when they'd be able to take over some of her burdens, things pressing down on her from society and in the family. Her sons grew up strong as bears and alert as eagles, but they never paid any attention to her. Her only recourse was to love them in silence, sadly, fearful of losing them. Later still, when they reached full maturity and things grew more difficult, her nature hardened. Since they obviously had no consideration for her at all, she hated them sometimes. Yet she because even more dependent upon their love, and that weakened her. Her fear of them had increased because all it took was a sign, a word, the sight of them, to dissolve her heart. But now she'd lost that fear. It no longer was crucial to her how they regarded her; their feelings were just not that important anymore. But didn't she love them now? Did she despise them? No, not a bit. She just saw them from a heightened perspective. When her sons talked to her about fighting Japs, she actually felt her love rekindle and was intensely pleased that the hardships she'd suffered rearing them had been worthwhile.

Slowly her daughters-in-law also stopped looking at her askance. Painful recollections and hopes for the future brought the women closer each day, harmonizing their relationships. When the women were alone, they always returned to the same topic of conversation. The frequent bickering that had afflicted the family before disappeared now, replaced by a new love founded on a common idea. The family found a closeness and unity it had never known before. And none of them ever realized that it was all the doing of the old lady.

VI

The sons came home with unusual news. Some people wanted to talk to her. More than likely it was because of her conduct. Little Jingu held her Granny's hand tightly as her Granny reassured her.

"Don't be scared, Granddaughter. Who could treat me worse than the Japs already did? I've taken the worst a body could. If I'm not even afraid of Hell anymore, what's there to be afraid of?"

"What the hell business is it of theirs?" Eldest Daughter-in-law said angrily. "Do you mean we can't even talk? No one ever said 'Chinese are lousy; Japs are great.' Shoot! They can take it and shove it!"

But why did they want to see her? Her son couldn't say

for sure. All he said was that someone had come from the Association looking for him, asking if she were his mother and what their address was, but that's all anyone knew about it. He wasn't real clear on what was going on, but he was pretty sure it was nothing to worry about.

The news made them rather uneasy. No stranger had ever come to call on her in her entire life. But she didn't lose any sleep over it that night. She really didn't care much about that sort of thing anymore.

The next day two women came over, one wearing a short jacket like the old woman's, the other, hair bobbed, in a uniform. They were both quite young. Without even a nod to conventional politeness, the old woman asked them in. They spoke first.

"Well, Mother," one of them addressed her in terms of special respect, "you may not know me, but I've known you for a long time. Twice I've heard you giving speeches."

"Speech." She didn't understand the word "speech" and just grunted glumly.[9]

"When I heard you speak, really, I couldn't help crying. Mother, since the Japs got hold of you, you must have seen everything you talk about with your own eyes, right?"

Her expression got friendlier. She thought, "Aha! They've finally come for news." And she began talking in an unending flood of words. They listened patiently to the greater part of the story. "Oh yes, Mother, we're with you on everything," they said when they were able to get a word in edgewise. "We too hate Japs with everything we've got. We try like mad to get people to join up and avenge the Chinese people, but we simply can't speak the way you can. Join our Association, Mother. Our Association tries to tell people these things in order to strike a blow against the Japs . . ."

"Jingu." Without waiting for them to finish, the old lady called her granddaughter, "Jingu, they've come to invite us to join their 'Association.' What do you say to that?" Without waiting for Jingu's reply, she turned back to her visitors. "I don't understand all that stuff," she said. "If you want me, I'll join. I'm not afraid you're just playing tricks on me, either. Two of my three sons joined the guerrillas and the other's in the Peasant Association. So it's all right if I join an association too. I won't lose anything by it, no matter what. Only if I join, my granddaughter has to join too."

They gave Jingu an enthusiastic welcome on the spot and offered the same to the two daughters-in-law.

The Women's Association expanded its membership rapidly after the old woman joined it. She went around every day recruiting, and once the women learned she was a member herself, they all wanted in. And so the women began to do quite a lot of work. Because of this, the old lady felt happier and seemed younger physically and in spirit. One day they decided to hold a big meeting in honor of the victories won by the guerrillas during the last three months. The meeting would take place at the same time as the celebration of International Women's Day on the eighth of March, and women's groups from nearby villages were invited to participate.

On the day of the rally, the old lady led several dozen women from Xiliu Village. Some carried their children; others led them by the hand. But they had not gathered to chat about children. They talked about their work responsibilities. A large number whose feet were bound had walked all the way, only barely aware of their pain and fatigue.

Quite a few had already arrived at the meeting place. The old woman's sons had come too, and many of her acquaintances waved to her from here and there. Gradually all the attention gave her a new feeling, a kind of uneasiness. It resembled shyness but was, in fact, the pride of accomplishment. After a little while, she felt calm again.

Slowly the crowd swelled. To the old woman it looked like a wave rolling in, and she was filled with happiness. So! They've got this many people!

The meeting began. Someone was speaking from the platform. The old woman listened raptly. It seemed to her that the speaker didn't waste a word. Who, listening to this speech, would not be moved by it? How could anyone listening fail to be concerned about the nation? Then they wanted her up on the platform.

When she heard their invitation, she was seized with unspeakable shyness and embarrassment. But her courage returned at once, and tottering a little, she walked to the podium on a wave of applause. Standing on high gazing downward, all she could see was a great mass of densely packed heads stretching out as far as the distant village wall, each with a face looking up at her. She felt rather stunned and giddy: What should I say, she thought. So she began by talking about herself.

"I am an old woman who was molested by the Japanese Imperialist troops. Look, all of you . . ." And she rolled up her sleeves to show her scars. "What are you scared of?" she said, hearing a murmur of sympathy from below. "This? This is nothing. . . ." Then she described the circumstances of her humiliation in plain, cold language, not trying to save her own face or hide her pain or spare their sensitivities. Her gaze roamed over their faces. They looked miserable! So she shouted, "Don't pity me! You should really pity yourselves! And protect yourselves! Today you think that I am the only one to be pitied. But, today, if you don't rise up, stand up to the Japs . . . ha! Heaven! I really don't want to see you suffer the way I did . . . I'm old, after all. A little more suffering is nothing to me: when I die, that's that, and so what. But look at you, how young you are! You should go on living. You haven't enjoyed what life has to offer. Can you have been born just to suffer, just to get pushed around by Japs?"

"We want to live!" Hundreds of voices shouted in anguish, "We weren't put here for the Japs to degrade and humiliate!"

She took over the burden of pain from those voices. She felt overwhelmed by something. At that instant she had only one desire: to sacrifice herself for their gratification. "I love all of you the same as I love my own sons," she shouted, "I'd die for you; but the Japs would never be satisfied with just me. They want you. They want every place, everywhere. Even a million me's wouldn't be enough to save you. You've got to save yourselves. If you want to stay alive, you'd better find a way to do it. . . . Before, I wasn't even willing to let my sons go out the door, much less fight. Now they're all guerrillas. They might get killed one day, but if they hadn't joined up, they would die even sooner. As long as there are those who can drive away Japs for everyone's sake, I wouldn't mind even if my own sons got killed. And if one of them dies, I'll remember him, you'll remember him, because he did it for all of us!"

Words gushed out of her like a wellspring. She couldn't think of how to stop them even when her excitement began flagging, and she couldn't stand straight any longer; her voice hoarsened, making it hard to shout. But the roar of applause went on and on. They wanted more.

At each shout the sea of heads broke into billows, like waves on the shore. Finally the old woman gathered all her remaining strength: "We must fight to the end!" An enormous roar answered her, the sound of a tidal wave crashing on the beach in a storm.

Leaning against arms that had come to prop her up, she gazed at the seething mass below. She felt an intimate awareness of something very powerful. Slowly she raised her eyes and looked above their heads to the vast open space, the endless blue sky. She saw the collapse of the old, the radiance of the new, and though tears blurred her vision, it was a radiance that sprang from her own steadfast faith.

Translated by Jean James and Tani E. Barlow

NOTES

1. The village of West Willow. Other names that transmit meaning include those of the three Chen brothers: Chen Xinhan or "Renew Han China" Chen, Chen Zuohan or "Aid the Han Chinese" Chen, and Chen Lihan or "Establish the Han Chinese" Chen.

2. A *mantou* is a steamed roll made of wheat and eaten in the North as daily bread.

3. The men refer to him as Zhang Laoyeh, a title that is both familiar and respectful.

4. The name in Chinese is Chen Dashu, the second term signifying that Chen belongs to (but is substantially younger than) the generation of the speaker's father.

5. In Northern dialect, this means "Second Brother."

6. Jingu means "Gold Daughter."

7. Laolao, "Granny," is the familiar term for one's maternal grandmother.

8. "Home of Respect for the Aged" is a euphemism for a labor camp.

9. The cadres, including art workers like Ding Ling, introduced the vocabulary of political propaganda and empowerment into village life. Among these words and behaviors was "speechifying."

LU HSUN

WHAT HAPPENS AFTER
NORA LEAVES HOME?

*A Talk Given at the Beijing
Women's Normal College, December 26, 1923*

My subject today is: What happens after Nora leaves home?

Ibsen was a Norwegian writer in the second half of the nineteenth century. All his works, apart from a few dozen poems, are dramas. Most of the dramas he wrote during one period deal with social problems and are known as social-problem plays. One of these is the play *Nora*.[1]

Another title for *Nora* is *Ein Puppenheim*, translated in Chinese as *A Puppet's House*. However, "puppe" are not only marionettes but also children's dolls; in a wider sense the term also includes people whose actions are controlled by others. Nora originally lives contentedly in a so-called happy home, but then she wakes up to the fact that she is simply a puppet of her husband's and her children are her puppets. So she leaves home—as the door is heard closing, the curtain falls. Since presumably you all know this play, there is no need to go into the details.

What could keep Nora from leaving? Some say that Ibsen himself has supplied the answer in *The Lady from the Sea*. The heroine of this play is married but her former lover, who lives just across the sea, seeks her out suddenly to ask her to elope with him. She tells her husband that she wants to meet this man and finally her husband says, "I give you complete freedom. Choose for yourself (whether to go or not). On your own head be it." This changes everything and she decides not to go. It seems from this that if Nora were to be granted similar freedom she might perhaps stay at home.

But Nora still goes away. What becomes of her afterwards Ibsen does not say, and now he is dead. Even if he were still living, he would not be obliged to give an answer. For Ibsen was writing poetry, not raising a problem for society and supplying the answer to it. This is like the golden oriole which sings because it wants to, not to amuse or benefit anyone else. Ibsen was rather lacking in worldly wisdom. It is said that when a number of women gave a banquet in his honor and their representative rose to thank him for writing *Nora*, which gave people a new insight into the social consciousness and emancipation of women, he rejoined, "I didn't write with any such ideas in mind, I was only writing poetry."

What happens after Nora leaves home? Others have also voiced their views on this. An Englishman has written a play about a modern woman who leaves home but finds no road open to her and therefore goes to the bad, ending up in a brothel. There is also a Chinese—how shall I describe him? A Shanghai man of letters, I suppose—who claims to have read a different version of the play in which Nora returns home in the end. Unfortunately no one else ever saw this edition, unless it was one sent him by Ibsen himself. But by logical deduction, Nora actually has two alternatives only: to go to the bad or to return to her husband. It is like the case of a caged bird: of course there is no freedom in the cage, but if it leaves the cage there are hawks, cats, and other hazards outside; while if imprisonment has atrophied its wings, of if it has forgotten how to fly, there certainly is nowhere it can go. Another alternative is to starve to death, but since that means departing this life it presents no problem and no solution either.

The most painful thing in life is to wake up from a dream and find no way out. Dreamers are fortunate people. If no way out can be seen, the important thing is not to awaken the sleepers. Look at the Tang Dynasty poet Li He whose whole life was dogged by misfortune. When he lay dying he said to his mother, "The Emperor of Heaven has built a palace of white jade, Mother, and summoned me there to write something to celebrate its completion." What was this if not a lie, a dream? But this made it possible for the young man who was dying to die happily, and for the old woman who lived on to set her heart at rest. At such times there is something great about lying and dreaming. To my mind, then, if we can find no way out, what we need are dreams.

However, it won't do to dream about the future. In one

of his novels Artzybashev[2] challenges those idealists who, in order to build a future golden world, call on many people here and now to suffer. "You promise their descendents a golden world, but what are you giving them themselves?" he demands. Something is given, of course—hope for the future. But the cost is exorbitant. For the sake of this hope, people are made more sensitive to the intensity of their misery, are awakened in spirit to see their own putrid corpses. At such times there is greatness only in lying and dreaming. To my mind, then, if we can find no way out, what we need are dreams; but not dreams of the future, just dreams of the present.

However, since Nora has awakened it is hard for her to return to the dream world; hence all she can do is to leave. After leaving, though, she can hardly avoid going to the bad or returning. Otherwise the question arises: What has she taken away with her apart from her awakened heart? If she has nothing but a crimson woolen scarf of the kind you young ladies are wearing, even if two or three feet wide it will prove completely useless. She needs more than that, needs something in her purse. To put it bluntly, what she needs is money.

Dreams are fine; otherwise money is essential.

The word money has an ugly sound. Fine gentlemen may scoff at it, but I believe that men's views often vary, not only from day to day but from before a meal to after it. All who admit that food costs money yet call money filthy lucre will probably be found, on investigation, to have some fish or pork not yet completely digested in their stomachs. You should hear their views again after they have fasted for a day.

Thus the crucial thing for Nora is money or—to give it a more high-sounding name—economic resources. Of course money cannot buy freedom, but freedom can be sold for money. Human beings have one great drawback, which is that they often get hungry. To remedy this drawback and to avoid being puppets, the most important thing in society today seems to be economic rights. First, there must be a fair sharing out between men and women in the family; secondly, men and women must have equal rights in society.

Unfortunately I have no idea how we are to get hold of these rights; all I know is that we have to fight for them. We may even have to fight harder for these than for political rights.

The demand for economic rights is undoubtedly something very commonplace, yet it may involve more difficulties than the demand for noble political rights or for the grand emancipation of women. In this world countless small actions involve more difficulties than big actions do. In a winter like this, for instance, if we have only a single padded jacket we must choose between saving a poor man from freezing to death or sitting like Buddha under a bo-tree to ponder ways of saving all mankind. The difference between saving all mankind and saving one individual is certainly vast. But given the choice I would not hesitate to sit down under the bo-tree, for that would obviate the need to take off my only padded jacket and freeze to death myself. This is why, at home, if you demand political rights you will not meet with much opposition, whereas if you speak about the equal distribution of wealth you will probably find yourself up against enemies, and this of course will lead to bitter fighting.

Fighting is not a good thing and we can't ask everybody to be a fighter. In that case the peaceful method is best, that is using parental authority to liberate one's children in future. Since in China parental authority is absolute, you can share out your property fairly among your children so that they enjoy equal economic rights in peace, free from conflict. They can then go to study, start a business, enjoy themselves, do something for society, or spend the lot just as they please, responsible to no one but themselves. Though this is also a rather distant dream, it is much closer than the dream of a golden age. But the first prerequisite is a good memory. A bad memory is an advantage to its owner but injurious to his descendents. The ability to forget the past enables people to free themselves gradually from the pain they once suffered; but it also often makes them repeat the mistakes of their predecessors. When a cruelly treated daughter-in-law becomes a mother-in-law, she may still treat her daughter-in-law cruelly; officials who detest students were often students who denounced officials; some parents who oppress their children now were probably rebels against their own families ten years ago. This perhaps has something to do with one's age and status; still bad memory is also a big factor here. The remedy for this is for everyone to buy a notebook and record his thoughts and actions from day to day, to serve as reference materials in future when his age and status have changed. If you are annoyed with your child for wanting to go to the park, you can look through your notes and find an entry saying, "I want to go to the Central Park." This will at once mollify and calm you down. The same applies to other matters too.

There is a kind of hooliganism today, the essence of which is tenacity. It is said that after the Boxer Uprising some ruffians in Tianjin behaved quite lawlessly. For instance, if one were to carry luggage for you, he would demand two dollars. If you argued that it was a small piece of luggage, he would demand two dollars. If you argued that the distance was short, he would demand two dollars. If you said you didn't need him, he would still demand two dollars. Of course hooligans are not good models, yet that tenacity is most admirable. It is the same in demanding economic rights. If someone says this is old hat, tell him you want your economic rights. If he says this is too low, tell him you want your economic rights. If he says the economic system will soon be changing and there is no need to worry, tell him you want your economic rights.

Actually, today, if just one Nora left home she might not find herself in difficulties; because such a case, being so exceptional, would enlist a good deal of sympathy and certain people would help her out. To live on the sympathy of others already means having no freedom; but if a hundred Noras were to leave home, even that sympathy would diminish; while if a thousand or ten thousand were to leave, they would arouse disgust. So having economic power in your own hands is far more reliable.

Are you not a puppet then when you have economic freedom? No, you are still a puppet. But you will be less at the beck and call of others and able to control more puppets yourself. For in present-day society it is not just women who are often the puppets of men; men often control other men, and women other women, while men are often women's puppets too. This is not something which can be remedied by a few women's possession of economic rights. However, people with empty stomachs cannot wait quietly for the arrival of a golden age; they must at least husband their last breath just as a fish in a dry rut flounders about to find a little water. So we need this relatively attainable economic power before we can devise other measures.

Of course, if the economic system changes then all this is empty talk.

In speaking as I have, however, I have assumed Nora to be an ordinary woman. If she is someone exceptional who prefers to dash off to sacrifice herself, that is a different matter. We have no right to urge people to sacrifice themselves, no right to stop them either. Besides, there are many people in the world who delight in self-sacrifice and suffering. In Europe there is a legend that when Jesus was on his way to be crucified he rested under the eaves of Ahasuerus' house, and because Ahasuerus turned Jesus away he became accursed, doomed to find no rest until the Day of Judgment. So since then Ahasuerus has been wandering, unable to rest, and he is still wandering now. Wandering is painful while resting is comfortable, so why doesn't he stop to rest? Because even if under a curse he must prefer wandering to resting; that is why he keeps up this frenzied wandering.

But this choice of sacrifice is a personal one which has nothing in common with the social commitment of revolutionaries. The masses, especially in China, are always spectators at a drama. If the victim on the stage acts heroically, they are watching a tragedy; if he shivers and shakes they are watching a comedy. Before the mutton shops in Beijing a few people often gather to gape, with evident enjoyment, at the skinning of the sheep. And this is all they get out of it if a man lays down his life. Moreover, after walking a few steps away from the scene they forget even this modicum of enjoyment.

There is nothing you can do with such people; the only way to save them is to give them no drama to watch. Thus there is no need for spectacular sacrifices; it is better to have persistent, tenacious struggle.

Unfortunately China is very hard to change. Just to move a table or overhaul a stove probably involves shedding blood; and even so, the change may not get made. Unless some great whip lashes her on the back, China will never budge. Such a whip is bound to come, I think. Whether good or bad, this whipping is bound to come. But where it will come from or how it will come I do not know exactly.

And here my talk ends.

NOTES

1. Chinese translation for *A Doll's House*.

2. Russian novelist (1878–1927).

DING LING

THOUGHTS ON MARCH 8

—

When will it no longer be necessary to attach special weight to the word "woman" and raise it specially?

Each year this day comes round. Every year on this day, meetings are held all over the world where women muster their forces. Even though things have not been as lively these last two years in Yan'an as they were in previous years, it appears that at least a few people are busy at work here. And there will certainly be a congress, speeches, circular telegrams, and articles.

Women in Yan'an are happier than women elsewhere in China. So much so that many people ask enviously: "How come the women comrades get so rosy and fat on millet?" It doesn't seem to surprise anyone that women make up a big proportion of the staff in the hospitals, sanatoria, and clinics, but they are inevitably the subject of conversation, as a fascinating problem, on every conceivable occasion.

Moreover, all kinds of women comrades are often the

target of deserved criticism. In my view these reproaches are serious and justifiable.

People are always interested when women comrades get married, but that is not enough for them. It is virtually impossible for women comrades to get onto friendly terms with a man comrade, and even less likely for them to become friendly with more than one. Cartoonists ridicule them: "A departmental head getting married too?" The poets say, "All the leaders in Yan'an are horsemen, and none of them are artists. In Yan'an it's impossible for an artist to find a pretty sweetheart." But in other situations, they are lectured: "Damn it, you look down on us old cadres and say we're country bumpkins. But if it weren't for us country bumpkins, you wouldn't be coming to Yan'an to eat millet!" But women invariably want to get married. (It's even more of a sin not to be married, and single women are even more of a target for rumors and slanderous gossip.) So they can't afford to be choosy, anyone will do: whether he rides horses or wears straw sandals, whether he's an artist or a supervisor. The inevitably have children. The fate of such children is various. Some are wrapped in soft baby wool and patterned felt and looked after by governesses. Others are wrapped in soiled cloth and left crying in their parents' beds, while their parents consume much of the child allowance. But for this allowance (twenty-five yuan a month, or just over three pounds of pork), many of them would probably never get a taste of meat. Whoever they marry, the fact is that those women who are compelled to bear children will probably be publicly derided as "Noras who have returned home." Those women comrades in a position to employ governesses can go out once a week to a prim get-together and dance. Behind their backs there will also be the most incredible gossip and whispering campaigns, but as soon as they go somewhere, they cause a great stir and all eyes are glued to them. This has nothing to do with our theories, our doctrines, and the speeches we make at meetings. We all know this to be a fact, a fact that is right before our eyes, but it is never mentioned.

It is the same with divorce. In general there are three conditions to pay attention to when getting married: (1) political purity; (2) both parties should be more or less the same age and comparable in looks; (3) mutual help. Even though everyone is said to fulfill these conditions—as for point 1, there are no open traitors in Yan'an; as for point 3, you can call anything "mutual help," including darning socks, patching shoes, and even feminine comfort—everyone nevertheless makes a great show of giving thoughtful attention to them. And yet the pretext for divorce is invariably the wife's political backwardness. I am the first to admit that it is a shame when a man's wife is not progressive and retards his progress. But let us consider to what degree they are backward. Before marrying, they were inspired by the desire to soar to the heavenly heights and lead a life of bitter struggle. They got married partly because of physiological necessity and partly as a response to sweet talk about "mutual help." Thereupon they are forced to toil away and become "Noras returned home." Afraid of being thought "backward," those who are a bit more daring rush around begging nurseries to take their children. They ask for abortions and risk punishment and even death by secretly swallowing potions to produce abortions. But the answer comes back: "Isn't giving birth to children also work? You're just after an easy life; you want to be in the limelight. After all, what indispensable political work have you performed? Since you are so frightened of having children and are not willing to take responsibility once you have had them, why did you get married in the first place? No one forced you to." Under these conditions, it is impossible for women to escape this destiny of "backwardness." When women capable of working sacrifice their careers for the joys of motherhood, people always since their praises.[1] But after ten years or so, they have no way of escaping the tragedy of "backwardness."[2] Even from my point of view, as a woman, there is nothing attractive about such "backward" elements. Their skin is beginning to wrinkle, their hair is growing thin, and fatigue is robbing them of their last traces of attractiveness. It should be self-evident that they are in a tragic situation. But whereas in the old society they would probably have been pitied and considered unfortunate, nowadays their tragedy is seen as something self-inflicted, as their just desserts. Is it not so that there is a discussion going on in legal circles as to whether divorces should be granted simply on the petition of one party or on the basis of mutual agreement? In the great majority of cases, it is the husband who petitions for divorce.[3]

For the wife to do so, she must be leading an immoral life, and then of course she deserves to be cursed.

I myself am a woman, and I therefore understand the failings of women better than others.[4] But I also have a deeper understanding of what they suffer. Women are incapable of transcending the age they live in, of being perfect, or of being hard as steel. They are incapable of resisting all the temptations of society or all the silent oppression they suffer here in Yan'an. They each have their own past written in blood and tears; they have experienced great emotions—in elation as in depression, whether engaged in the lone battle of life or drawn into the humdrum stream of life. This is even truer of the women comrades who come to Yan'an, and I therefore have much sympathy for those fallen and classified as criminals. What is more, I hope that men, especially those in top positions, as well as women themselves, will consider the mistakes women commit in their social context. It would be better if there were less empty theorizing and more talk about real problems, so that theory and practice would not be divorced, and better if all Communist Party members were more responsible for their own moral conduct.[5] But we must also hope for a little more from our women comrades, especially those in Yan'an. We must urge ourselves on and develop our comradely feeling.

People without ability have never been in a position to seize everything. Therefore, if women want equality, they must first strengthen themselves. There is no need to stress this point, since we all understand it. Today there are certain to be people who make fine speeches bragging about the need to acquire political power first. I would simply mention a few things that any frontliner, whether a proletarian, a fighter in the war of resistance, or a woman, should pay attention to in his or her everyday life:

1. Don't allow yourself to fall ill. A wild life can at times appear romantic, poetic, and attractive, but in today's conditions it is inappropriate. You are the best keeper of your life. There is nothing more unfortunate nowadays that to lose your health. It is closest to your heart. The only thing to so is keep a close watch on it, pay careful attention to it, and cherish it.

2. Make sure you are happy. Only when you are happy can you be youthful, active, fulfilled in your life, and steadfast in the face of all difficulties; only then will you see a future ahead of you and know how to enjoy yourself. This sort of happiness is not a life of contentment, but a life of struggle and of advance. Therefore we should all do some meaningful work each day and some reading, so that each of us is in a position to give something to others. Loafing about simply encourages the feeling that life is hollow, feeble, and in decay.

3. Use your brain, and make a habit of doing so. Correct any tendency not to think and ponder, or to swim with the current. Before you say or do anything, think whether what you are saying is right, whether that is the most suitable way of dealing with the problem, whether it goes

against your own principles, whether you feel you can take responsibility for it. Then you will have no cause to regret your actions later.[6] This is what is known as acting rationally. It is the best way of avoiding the pitfalls of sweet words and honeyed phrases, of being sidetracked by petty gains, of wasting our emotions and wasting our lives.

4. Resolution in hardship, perseverance to the end. Aware, modern women should identify and cast off all their rosy illusions. Happiness is to take up the struggle in the midst of the raging storm and not to pluck the lute in the moonlight or recite poetry among the blossoms. In the absence of the greatest resolution, it is very easy to falter in mid path. Not to suffer is to become degenerate. The strength to carry on should be nurtured through the quality of "perseverance." People without great aims and ambitions rarely have the firmness of purpose that does not covet petty advantages or seek a comfortable existence. But only those who have aims and ambitions for the benefit, not of the individual, but of humankind as a whole can persevere to the end.

August 3, dawn

POSTSCRIPT

On rereading this article, it seems to me that there is much room for improvement in the passage on what we should expect from women, but because I have to meet a deadline with the manuscript, I have no time to revise it. But I also feel that there are some things that, if said by a leader before a big audience, would probably evoke satisfaction. But when they are written by a woman, they are more than likely to be demolished. But since I have written it, I offer it as I always intended, for the perusal of those people who have similar views.

Translated by Gregor Benton

NOTES

1. The more literal rendering of this line is as follows: "When a woman capable of work sacrifices her career and becomes a 'virtuous wife, good mother' [*xianchi liangmu*] everybody sings her praises." This of course was the hated stereotype of domestic femininity that May Fourth radicals attacked so violently.

2. The "tragedy of backwardness" is, of course, divorce.

3. This was simply not true among peasants. Outside the revolutionary elite, divorce was the daughter-in-law's tool against an abusive mother-in-law and the wife's second greatest threat against her husband. The first was suicide.

4. The word in the text is, once again, *quedian*. For other uses of this word to describe women's failings see *Shanghai, Spring 1930* and "Yecao."

5. This passage has been edited to achieve sex neutrality. The version of this translation published earlier read, "if each Communist Party member were more responsible for his own moral conduct." Since Chinese does not give pronouns a gender, my revision is in fact truer to the text.

6. The important term is *houwu*, "regret," a constant theme in the writer's earliest fiction.

LU HSUN

REGRET FOR THE PAST

Chuan-sheng's Notes

—

I want, if I can, to describe my remorse and grief for Tzu-chun's sake as well as for my own. This shabby room, tucked away in a forgotten corner of the hostel, is so quiet and empty. Time really flies. A whole year has passed since I fell in love with Tzu-chun, and, thanks to her, escaped from this dead quiet and emptiness. On my return, as ill luck would have it, this was the only room vacant. The broken window with the half dead locust tree and old wistaria outside and square table inside are the same as before. The same too are the moldering wall and wooden bed beside it. At night I lie in bed alone just as I did before I started living with Tzu-chun. The past year has been blotted out as if it had never been—as if I had never moved out of this shabby room so hopefully to set up a small home in Chichao Street.

Nor is that all. A year ago this silence and emptiness were different—there was often an expectancy about them. I was expecting Tzu-chun's arrival. As I waited long and impatiently, the tapping of high heels on the brick pavement would galvanize me into life. Then I would see her pale round face dimpling in a smile, her thin white arms, striped cotton blouse and black skirt. She would bring in a new leaf from the half withered locust tree outside the window for me to look at, or clusters of the mauve flowers that hung from the old wistaria tree, the trunk of which looked as if made of iron.

Now there is only the old silence and emptiness. Tzu-chun will not come again—never, never again.

In Tzu-chun's absence, I saw nothing in this shabby room. Out of sheer boredom I would pick up a book—science or literature, it was all the same to me—and read on and on, till I realized I had turned a dozen pages without taking in a word I had read. Only my ears were so sensitive, I seemed able to hear all the footsteps outside the gate, those of Tzu-chun among the rest. Her steps often sounded as if they were drawing nearer and nearer—only to grow fainter again, until they were lost in the tramping of other feet. I hated the servant's son who wore cloth-soled shoes which sounded quite different from Tzu-chun's. I hated the pansy next door who used face cream, who often wore new leather shoes, and whose steps sounded all too like Tzu-chun's.

Had her rickshaw been upset? Had she been knocked over by a tram? . . .

I would be on the point of putting on my hat to go and see her, then remember her uncle had cursed me to my face.

Suddenly I would hear her coming nearer step by step, and by the time I was out to meet her she would already have passed the wistaria trellis, her face dimpling in a smile. Probably she wasn't badly treated after all in her uncle's home. I would calm down and, after we had gazed at each other in silence for a moment, the shabby room would be filled with the sound of my voice as I held forth on the tyranny of the home, the need to break with tradition, the equality of men and women, Ibsen, Tagore and Shelley. . . . She would nod her head, smiling, her eyes filled with a childlike look of wonder. On the wall was nailed a copperplate bust of Shelley, cut out from a magazine. It was one of the best likenesses of him, but when I pointed it out to her she only gave it a hasty glance, then hung her head as if embarrassed. In matters like this, Tzu-chun probably hadn't yet freed herself entirely from old ideas. It occurred to me later it might be better to substitute a picture of Shelley being drowned at sea, or a portrait of Ibsen. But I never got round to it. Now even this picture has vanished.

"I'm my own mistress. None of them has any right to interfere with me."

She came out with this statement clearly, firmly and gravely, after a thoughtful silence—we had been talking about her uncle who was here and her father who was at home. We had then known each other for half a year. I had already told her all my views, all that had happened to me, and what my failings were. I had hidden very little, and she understood me completely. These few words of hers stirred me to the bottom of my heart, and rang in my ears for many days after. I was unspeakably happy to know that Chinese women were not as hopeless as the pessimists made out, and that we should see them in the not too distant future in all their glory.

Each time I saw her out, I always kept several paces behind her. The old man's face with its whiskers like fishy tentacles was always pressed hard against the dirty window-pane, so that even the tip of his nose was flattened. When we reached the outer courtyard, against the bright glass window there was that little fellow's face, plastered with face cream. But walking out proudly, without looking right or left, Tzu-chun did not see them. And I walked proudly back.

"I'm my own mistress. None of them has any right to interfere with me." Her mind was completely made up on this point. She was by far the more thoroughgoing and reso-lute of the two of us. What did she care about the half pot of face cream or the flattened nose tip?

I can't remember clearly now how I expressed my true, passionate love for her. Not only now—even just after it happened, my impression was very blurred. When I thought back at night, I could only remember snatches of what I had said; while during the month or two after we started living together, even these fragments vanished like a dream without a trace. I only remember how for about a fortnight beforehand I had reflected very carefully what attitude to adopt, prepared what to say, and decided what to do if I were refused. But when the time came it was all no use. In my nervousness, I unconsciously did what I had seen in the movies. The memory of this makes me thoroughly ashamed, yet this is the one thing I remember clearly. Even today it is like a solitary lamp in a dark room, lighting me up. I clasped her hand with tears in my eyes, and went down on one knee. . . .

I did not even see clearly how Tzu-chun reacted at the time. All I know was that she accepted me. However, I seem to remember her face first turned pale then gradually flushed red—redder than I have ever seen it before or since. Sadness and joy flashed from her childlike eyes, mingled with apprehension, although she struggled to avoid my gaze, looking, in her confusion, as if she would like to fly out of the window. Then I knew she consented, although I didn't know what she said, or whether she said anything at all.

She, however, remembered everything. She could recite all that I said non-stop, as if she had learned it by heart. She described all of my actions in detail, to the life, like a film unfolding itself before my eyes, which included, naturally, that shallow scene from the movies which I was anxious to forget. At night, when all was still, it was our time for review. I was often questioned and examined, or ordered to retell all that had been said on that occasion; but she often had to fill up gaps and correct my mistakes, as if I were a Grade D student.

Gradually these reviews became few and far between. But whenever I saw her gazing raptly into space with a tender look and dimpling, I knew she was going over that old lesson again, and would be afraid she was seeing my ridiculous act from the movies. I knew, though, that she did see it, and that she insisted on seeing it.

But she didn't find it ridiculous. Though I thought it laughable, even contemptible, she didn't find it so at all. And I knew this was because she loved me so truly and passionately.

Late spring last year was our happiest and busiest time. I was calmer then, although one part of my mind became as active as my body. This was when we started going out together. We went several times to the park, but more often to look for lodgings. On the road I was conscious of searching looks, sarcastic smiles or lewd and contemptuous glances which tended, if I was not careful, to make me shiver. Every instant I had to summon all my pride and defiance to my support. She was quite fearless, however, and completely impervious to all this. She proceeded slowly, as calmly as if there were nobody in sight.

To find lodgings was no easy matter. In most cases we were refused on some pretext, while some places we were turned down as unsuitable. In the beginning we were very particular—and yet not too particular either, because most of these lodgings were not places where we could live. Later on, all we asked was to be tolerated. We looked at over twenty places before we found one we could make do—two rooms facing north in a small house on Chichao Street. The owner of the house was a petty official, but an intelligent man, who only occupied the central and side rooms. His household consisted simply of a wife, a baby a few months old, and a maid from the country. As long as the child didn't cry, it would be very quiet.

Our furniture, simple as it was, had already taken the greater part of the money I had raised: and Tzu-chun had sold her only gold ring and ear-rings too. I tried to stop her, but she insisted, so I didn't press the point. I knew, if she hadn't a share in our home, she would feel uncomfortable.

She had already quarrelled with her uncle—in fact he was so angry that he disowned her. I had also broken with several friends who thought they were giving me good advice but were actually either afraid for me, or jealous. Still, this meant we were very quiet. Although it was nearly dark when I left the office, and the rickshaw man went so slowly, the time finally came when we were together again. First we would look at each other in silence, then relax and talk intimately, and finally fall silent again, bowing our heads without think-ing of anything in particular. Gradually I was able to read her soberly like a book, body and soul. In a mere three weeks I learned much more about her, and broke down barriers which I had not known existed, but then discovered had been real barriers.

As the days passed, Tzu-chun became more lively. How-ever, she didn't like flowers. I bought two pots of flowers at the fair, but after four days without water they died neglected in a corner. I hadn't the time to see to everything. She had a liking for animals, though, which she may have picked up from the official's wife; and in less than a month our household was greatly increased. Four chicks of ours started picking their way across the courtyard with the landlady's dozen. But the two mistresses could tell them apart, each able to spot her own. Then there was a spotted dog, bought at the fair. I believe he had a name to begin with, but Tzu-chun gave him a new one—Ahsui. I called him Ahsui too, though I didn't like the name.

It is true that love must be constantly renewed, must grow and create. When I spoke of this to Tzu-chun, she nodded understandingly.

Ah, what peaceful, happy evenings those were!

Tranquility and happiness must be consolidated, so that they may last for ever. When we were in the hostel, we had occasional differences of opinion or misunderstandings; but after we moved into Chichao Street even these slight differences vanished. We just sat opposite each other in the lamplight, reminiscing, savouring again the joy of the new harmony which had followed our disputes.

Tzu-chun grew plumper and her cheeks became rosier; the only pity was she was too busy. Her house-keeping left her no time even to chat, much less to read or go out for walks. We often said we would have to get a maid.

Another thing that upset me when I got back in the evening, was to see her try to hide a look of unhappiness or—and this depressed me even more—force a smile on to her face. Luckily I had discovered this was due to her secret feud with the petty official's wife, and the bone of contention was the chicks. But why wouldn't she tell me? People ought to have a home of their own. This was no place to live in.

I had my routine too. Six days of the week I went from home to the office and from the office home. In the office I sat at my desk endlessly copying official documents and letters. At home I kept her company or helped her light the stove, cook rice or steam bread. This was when I learned to cook.

Still, I ate much better than when I was in the hostel. Although cooking was not Tzu-chun's strongest point, she threw herself into it heart and soul. Her ceaseless anxieties on this score made me anxious too, and in this way we shared the sweet and the bitter together. She kept at it so hard all day, perspiration made her short hair stick to her head, and her hands grew rough.

And then she had to feed Ahsui and the chicks . . . nobody else could do this.

I told her, I would rather not eat than see her work herself to the bone like this. She just gazed at me without a word, rather wistfully; and I couldn't very well say any more. Still she went on working as hard as ever.

Finally the blow I had been expecting fell. The evening before the Double Tenth Festival, I was sitting idle while she washed the dishes, when we heard a knock on the door. When I went to open it, I found the messenger from our office who handed me a mimeographed slip of paper. I guessed what it was, and when I took it to the lamp, sure enough, it read:

> By order of the commissioner, Shih Chuan-sheng
> is discharged.
>
> The secretariat,
> October 9th.

I had foreseen this while we were still in the hostel. That Face Cream was one of the gambling friends of the commissioner's son. He was bound to spread rumours and try to make trouble. I was only surprised this hadn't happened sooner. In fact this was really no blow, because I had already decided I could work as a clerk somewhere else or teach, or, although it was a little more difficult, do some translation work. I knew the editor of *Freedom's Friend*, and had corresponded with him a couple of months previously. All the same, my heart was thumping. What distressed me most was that even Tzu-chun, fearless as she was, had turned pale. Recently she seemed to have grown weaker.

"What does it matter?" she said. "We'll make a new start, won't we? We'll . . ."

She didn't finish, and her voice sounded flat. The lamplight seemed unusually dim. Men are really laughable creatures, so easily upset by trifles. First we gazed at each other in silence, then started discussing what to do. Finally we decided to live as economically as possible on the money we had, to advertise in the paper for a post as clerk or teacher, and to write at the same time to the editor of *Freedom's Friend*, explaining my present situation and asking him to accept a translation to help me out of this difficulty.

"As good said as done! Let's make a fresh start."

I went straight to the table and pushed aside the bottle of vegetable oil and dish of vinegar, while Tzu-chun brought over the dim lamp. First I drew up the advertisement; then I made a selection of books to translate. I hadn't looked at my books since we moved house, and each volume was thick with dust. Finally I wrote the letter.

I hesitated for a long time over the wording of the letter, and when I stopped writing to think, and glanced at her in the dusky lamplight, she was looking very wistful again. I had never imagined a trifle like this could cause such a striking change in someone so firm and fearless as Tzu-chun. She really had grown much weaker lately—it wasn't something that had just started that evening. This made me feel more put out. I had a sudden vision of a peaceful life—the quiet of my shabby room in the hostel flashed before my eyes, and I was just going to take a good look at it when I found myself back in the dusky lamplight again.

After a long time the letter was finished. It was very lengthy, and I was so tired after writing it, I realized I must have grown weaker myself lately too. We decided to send in the advertisement and post the letter the next day. Then with one accord we straightened up, silently, as if conscious of each other's fortitude and strength, and able to see new hope growing from this fresh beginning.

. . .

Actually, this blow from outside infused a new spirit into us. In the office I had lived like a wild bird in a cage, given just enough canary-seed by its captor to keep alive, but not to grow fat. As time passed it would lose the use of its wings, so that if ever it were let out of the cage it could no longer fly. Now, at any rate, I had got out of the cage, and must soar anew in the wide sky before it was too late, while I could still flap my wings.

Of course we could not expect results from a small advertisement right away. However, translating is not so simple either. You read something and think you understand it, but when you come to translate it difficulties crop up everywhere, and it's very slow going. Still, I determined to do my best. In less than a fortnight, the edge of a fairly new dictionary was black with my finger-prints, which showed how seriously I took my work. The editor of *Freedom's Friend* had said that his magazine would never ignore a good manuscript.

Unfortunately, there was no room where I could be undisturbed, and Tzu-chun was not as quiet or considerate as she had been. Our room was so cluttered up with dishes and bowls and filled with smoke, it was impossible to work steadily there. Of course I had only myself to blame for this—it was my fault for not being able to afford a study. On top of this there was Ahsui and the chicks. The chicks had grown into hens now, and were more of a bone of contention than ever between the two families.

Then there was the never-ending business of eating every day. All Tzu-chun's efforts seemed to be devoted to our meals. One ate to earn, and earned to eat; while Ahsui and the hens had to be fed too. Apparently she had forgotten all she had ever learned, and did not realize that she was interrupting my train of thought when she called me to meals. And although as I sat down I sometimes showed a little displeasure, she paid no attention at all, but just went on munching away quite unconcerned.

It took her five weeks to learn that my work could not be restricted by regular eating hours. When she did realize it she was probably annoyed, but she said nothing. After that my work did go forward faster, and soon I had translated 50,000 words. I had only to polish the manuscript, and it could be sent in with two already completed shorter pieces to *Freedom's Friend*. Those meals were still a headache though. It didn't matter if the dishes were cold, but there weren't enough of them. My appetite was much smaller than before, now that I was sitting at home all day using my brain, but even so there wasn't always even enough rice. It had been given to Ahsui, sometimes along with the mutton which recently, I myself had rarely a chance to eat. She said Ahsui was so thin, it was really pathetic, and it made the landlady sneer at us. She couldn't stand being laughed at.

So there were only the hens to eat my left-overs. It was a long time before I realized this. I was very conscious, however, that my "place in the universe," as Huxley describes it, was only somewhere between the dogs and the hens.

. . .

Later on, after much argument and insistence, the hens started appearing on our tale, and we and Ahsui were able to enjoy them for over ten days. They were very thin, though, because for a long time they had only been fed a few grains of *kaoliang* a day. After that life became much more peaceful. Only Tzu-chun was very dispirited, and seemed so sad and bored without them, she grew rather sulky. How easily people change!

However, Ahsui too would have to be given up. We had stopped hoping for a letter from anywhere, and for a long time Tzu-chun had had no food left to make the dog beg or stand on his hind legs. Besides, winter was coming on very fast, and we didn't know what to do about a stove. His appetite had long been a heavy liability, of which we were all too conscious. So even the dog had to go.

If we had tied a tag on him and taken him to the market to sell, we might have made a few coppers. But neither of us could bring ourselves to do this.

Finally I muffled his head in a cloth and took him outside the West Gate where I let him loose. When he ran after me, I pushed him into a pit that wasn't too deep.

When I got home, I found it more peaceful; but I was quite taken aback by Tzu-chun's tragic expression. I had never seen her so woebegone. Of course, it was because of Ahsui, but why take it so to heart? I didn't tell her about pushing him into the pit.

That night, something icy crept into her expression too.

"Really!" I couldn't help saying. "What's got into you today, Tzu-chun?"

"What?" She didn't even look at me.

"You look so . . ."

"It's nothing—nothing at all."

Eventually I realized she must consider me callous. Actually, when I was on my own I had got along very well, although I was too proud to mix much with family acquaintances. But since my move I had become estranged from all my old friends. Still, if I could only get away from all this, there were plenty of ways open to me. Now I had to put up with all these hardships mainly because of her—getting rid of Ahsui was a case in point. But Tzu-chun seemed too obtuse now even to understand that.

When I took an opportunity to hint this to her, she nodded as if she understood. But judging by her behaviour later, she either didn't take it in or else didn't believe me.

The cold weather and her cold looks made it impossible for me to be comfortable at home. But where could I go? I could get away from her icy looks in the street and parks, but the cold wind outside whistled through me. Finally I found a haven in the public library.

Admission was free, and there were two stoves in the reading room. Although the fire was very low, the mere sight of the stoves made me warm. There were no books worth reading: the old ones were out of date, and there were practically no new ones.

But I didn't go there to read. There were usually a few other people there, sometimes as many as a dozen, all thinly clad like me. We kept up a pretence of reading, in order to keep out of the cold. This suited me down to the ground. You were liable to meet people you knew on the road who would glance at you contemptuously, but here there was no trouble of that kind, because my acquaintances were all gathered round other stoves or warming themselves at the stoves in their own homes.

Although there were no books for me to read there, I found quiet in which to think. As I sat there alone thinking over the past, I felt that during the last half year for love— blind love—I had neglected all the important things in life. First and foremost, livelihood. A man must make a living before there can be any place for love. There must be a way out for those who struggle, and I hadn't yet forgotten how to flap my wings, though I was much weaker than before. . . .

The room and readers gradually faded. I saw fishermen in the angry sea, soldiers in the trenches, dignitaries in their cars, speculators at the stock exchange, heroes in mountain forests, teachers on their platforms, night prowlers, thieves in the dark. . . . Tzu-chun was far away. She had lost all her courage in her resentment over Ahsui and absorption in her cooking. The strange thing was that she didn't look particularly thin. . . .

It grew colder. The few lumps of slow-burning hard coal in the stove had at last burned out, and it was closing time. I had to go back to Chichao Street, to expose myself to that icy look. Of late I had sometimes been met with warmth, but this only upset me more. I remember one evening, the childlike look I had not seen for so long flashed from Tzu-chun's eyes as she reminded me with a smile of something that had happened at the hostel. But there was a constant look of fear in her eyes too. The fact that I had treated her more coldly recently than she had me worried her. Sometimes I forced myself to talk and laugh to comfort her. But the emptiness of my laughter and speech, and the way it immediately reechoed in my ears like a hateful sneer, was more than I could bear.

Tzu-chun might have felt it too, for after this she lost her wooden calm and, though she tried her best to hide it, often showed anxiety. She treated me, however, much more tenderly.

I wanted to speak to her plainly, but hadn't the courage. Whenever I made up my mind to speak, the sight of those childlike eyes compelled me, for the time being, to smile. But my smile turned straightaway into a sneer at myself, and made me lose my cold composure.

After that she revived the old questions and started new tests, forcing me to give all sorts of hypocritical answers to show my affection for her. Hypocrisy became branded on my heart, so filling it with falseness it was hard to breathe. I often felt, in my depression, that really great courage was needed to tell the truth; for a man who lacked courage and reconciled himself to hypocrisy would never find a new path. What's more, he just could not exist.

Then Tzu-chun started looking resentful. This happened for the first time one morning, one bitterly cold morning, or so I imagined. I smiled secretly to myself, cold with indignation. All the ideas and intelligent, fearless phrases she had learned were empty after all. Yet she did not know this. She had given up reading long ago, and did not realize the first thing in life is to make a living, that to do this people must advance hand in hand, or go forward singly. All she could do was cling to someone else's clothing, making it difficult even for a fighter to struggle, and bringing ruin on both.

I felt that our only hope lay in parting. She ought to make a clean break. Suddenly I thought of her death, but immediately was ashamed and reproached myself. Happily it was morning, and there was plenty of time for me to tell her the truth. Whether or not we could make a fresh start depended on this.

I deliberately brought up the past. I spoke of literature, then of foreign authors and their works, of Ibsen's *Nora* and *The Woman of the Sea*. I praised Nora for being strong-minded. . . . All this had been said the previous year in the shabby room in the hostel, but now it rang hollow. As the words left my mouth I could not free myself from the suspicion that there was an unseen urchin behind me maliciously parroting all I said.

She listened, nodding in agreement, then was silent. I finished what I had to say abruptly, and my voice died away in the emptiness.

"Yes," she said after another silence, "but . . . Chuan-sheng, I feel you've changed a lot lately. Is it true? Tell me!"

This was a blow, but I took a grip on myself, and explained my views and proposals: to make a fresh start and turn over a new leaf, to avoid being ruined together.

To clinch the matter, I said firmly:

". . . Besides, you need have no more scruples but go boldly ahead. You asked me to tell the truth. Yes, we shouldn't be hypocritical. Well, to tell the truth—it's because I don't love you anymore! Actually, this makes it better for you, because it'll be easier for you to work without any regret. . . ."

I was expecting a scene, but all that followed was silence. Her face turned ashy pale, like a corpse; but in a moment her color came back, and that childlike look darted from her eyes. She looked all round, like a hungry child searching for its kind mother, but only looked into space. Fearfully she avoided my eyes.

The sight was more than I could stand. Fortunately it was still early. I braved the cold wind to hurry to the library.

There I saw *Freedom's Friend*, with all my short articles in it. This took me by surprise, and seemed to bring me new life. "There are plenty of ways open to me," I thought. "But things can't go on like this."

I started calling on old friends with whom I had had nothing to do for a long time, but didn't go more than once or twice. Naturally, their rooms were warm, but I felt chilled to the marrow there. In the evenings I huddled in a room colder than ice.

An icy needle pierced my heart, making me suffer

continually from numb wretchedness. "There are plenty of ways open to me," I thought. "I haven't forgotten how to flap my wings." Suddenly I thought of her death, but immediately was ashamed and reproached myself.

In the library I often saw like a flash a new path ahead of me. I imagined she had faced up bravely to the facts and boldly left this icy home. Left it, what was more, without any malice towards me. Then I felt light as a cloud floating in the void, with the blue sky above and high mountains and great oceans below, big buildings and skyscrapers, battlefields, motorcars, thoroughfares, rich men's houses, bright, bustling markets, and the dark night. . . .

What's more, I really felt this new life was just around the corner.

Somehow we managed to live through the bitter Peking winter. But we were like dragonflies that had fallen into the hands of mischievous imps, been tied with threads, played with and tormented at will. Although we had come through alive, we were prostrate, and the end was only a matter of time.

Three letters were sent to the editor of *Freedom's Friend* before he replied. The envelope contained two book tokens, one for twenty cents, one for thirty cents. But I had spent nine cents on postage to press for payment, and gone hungry for a whole day, all for nothing.

However, I felt that at last I had got what I expected.

Winter was giving place to spring, and the wind was not quite so icy now. I spent more time wandering outside, and generally did not reach home till dusk. One dark evening, I came home listlessly as usual and, as usual, grew so depressed at the sight of our gate that I slowed down. Eventually, however, I reached my room. It was dark inside, and as I groped for the matches to strike a light, the place seemed extraordinarily quiet and empty.

I was standing there in bewilderment, when the official's wife called to me through the window.

"Tzu-chun's father came today," she said simply, "and took her away."

This was not what I had expected. I felt as if hit on the back of the head, and stood speechless.

"She went?" I finally managed to ask.

"Yes."

"Did—did she say anything?"

"No. Just asked me to tell you when you came back that she had gone."

I couldn't believe it; yet the room was so extraordinarily quiet and empty. I looked everywhere for Tzu-chun, but all I could see was the old, discolored furniture which appeared very scattered, to show that it was incapable of hiding anyone or anything. It occurred to me she might have left a letter or at least jotted down a few words, but no. Only salt, dried paprika, flour and half a cabbage had been placed together, with a few dozen coppers at the side. These were all our worldly goods, and now she had carefully left all this to me, bidding me without words to use this to eke out my existence a little longer.

Feeling my surroundings pressing in on me, I hurried out to the middle of the courtyard, where all around was dark. Bright lamplight showed on the window paper of the central rooms, where they were teasing the baby to make her laugh. My heart grew calmer, and I began to glimpse a way out of this heavy oppression: high mountains and great marshland, thoroughfares, brightly lit feasts, trenches, pitch-black night, the thurst of a sharp knife, noiseless footsteps. . . .

I relaxed, though about traveling expenses, and sighed.

I conjured up a picture of my future as I lay with closed eyes, but before the night was half over it had vanished. In the gloom I suddenly seemed to see a pile of groceries, then Tzu-chun's ashen face appeared to gaze at me beseechingly with childlike eyes. But as soon as I took a grip on myself, there was nothing there.

However, my heart still felt heavy. Why couldn't I have waited a few days instead of blurting out the truth like that to her? Now she knew all that was left to her was the passionate sternness of her father—who was as heartless as a creditor with his children—and the icy-cold looks of bystanders. Apart from this there was only emptiness. How terrible to bear the heavy burden of emptiness, treading one's life amid sternness and cold looks! And at the end not even a tombstone to your grave!

I shouldn't have told Tzu-chun the truth. Since we had loved each other, I should have gone on lying to her. If truth is a treasure, it shouldn't have proved such a heavy burden of emptiness to Tzu-chun. Of course, lies are empty too, but at least they wouldn't have proved so crushing a burden in the end.

I thought if I told Tzu-chun the truth, she could go forward boldly without scruples, just as when we started living together. But I was wrong. She was fearless then because of her love.

I hadn't the courage to shoulder the heavy burden of hypocrisy, so I thrust the burden of the truth on to her. Because she had loved me, she had to bear this heavy burden, amid sternness and cold glances to the end of her days.

I had thought of her death. . . . I realized I was a weakling. I deserved to be cast out by the strong, no matter whether they were truthful or hypocritical. Yet she, from first to last, had hoped that I could live longer. . . .

I wanted to leave Chichao Street; it was too empty and lonely here. I thought, if once I could get away, it would be as if Tzu-chun were still at my side. Or at least as if she were still in town, and might drop in on me any time, as she had when I lived in the hostel.

However, all my letters went unanswered, as did my applications to friends to find me a post. There was nothing for it but to go to see a family acquaintance I hadn't visited for a long time. This was an old classmate of my uncle's, a highly respected senior licentiate, who had lived in Peking for many years and had a wide circle of acquaintances.

The gatekeeper stared at me scornfully—no doubt

because my clothes were shabby—and only with difficulty was I admitted. My uncle's friend still remembered me, but treated me very coldly. He knew all about us.

"Obviously, you can't stay here," he said coldly, after I asked him to recommend me to a job somewhere else. "But where will you go? It's extremely difficult. That—er—that friend of yours, Tzu-chun, I suppose you know, is dead."

I was dumbfounded.

"Are you sure?" I finally blurted out.

He gave an artificial laugh. "Of course I am. My servant Wang Sheng comes from the same village as her family."

"But—how did she die?"

"Who knows? At any rate, she's dead."

I have forgotten how I took my leave and went home. I knew he wouldn't lie. Tzu-chun would never be with me again, as she had last year. Although she wanted to bear the burden of emptiness amid sternness and cold glances till the end of her days, it had been too much for her. Fate had decided that she should die knowing the truth I had told her—die unloved!

Obviously, I could not stay there. But where could I go?

All around was a great void, quiet as death. I seemed to see the darkness before the eyes of every single person who had died unloved, and to hear all the bitter and despairing cries of their struggle.

I was waiting for something new, something nameless and unexpected. But day after day passed in the same deadly quiet.

. . .

I went out now much less than before, sitting or lying in this great void, allowing this deathly quiet to eat away my soul. Sometimes the silence itself seemed afraid, seemed to recoil. At such times there would flash up nameless, unexpected, new hope.

One overcast morning, when the sun was unable to struggle out from behind the clouds and the very air was tired, the patter of tiny feet and a snuffling sound made me open my eyes. A glance around the room revealed nothing, but when I looked down I saw a small creature pattering around—thin, covered with dust, more dead than alive. . . .

When I looked harder, my heart missed a beat. I jumped up.

It was Ahsui. He had come back.

I left Chichao Street not just because of the cold glances of my landlord and the maid, but largely on account of Ahsui. But where could I go? I realized, naturally, there were many ways open to me, and sometimes seemed to see them stretching before me. I didn't know, though, how to take the first step.

After much deliberation, I decided the hostel was the only place where I could put up. Here is the same shabby room as before, the same wooden bed, half dead locust tree and wistaria. But what gave me love and life, hope and happiness before has vanished. There is nothing but emptiness, the empty existence I exchanged for the truth.

. . .

REGRET FOR THE PAST

There were many ways open to me, and I must take one of them because I am still living. I don't know, though, how to take the first step. Sometimes the road seems like a great, grey serpent, writhing and darting at me. I wait and wait and watch it approach, but it always disappears suddenly in the darkness.

The early spring nights are as long as ever. I sit idly for a long time and recall a funeral procession I saw on the street this morning. There were paper figures and paper horses in front, and behind crying that sounded like a lilt. I see how clever they are—this is so simple.

Then Tzu-chun's funeral springs to my mind. She bore the heavy burden of emptiness alone, advancing down the long grey road, only to be swallowed up amid sternness and cold glances.

I wish we really had ghosts and there really were a hell. Then, no matter how the wind of hell roared, I would go to find Tzu-chun, tell her of my remorse and grief, and beg her forgiveness. Otherwise, the poisonous flames of hell would surround me, and fiercely devour my remorse and grief.

In the whirlwind and flames I would put my arms around Tzu-chun, and ask her pardon, or try to make her happy. . . .

However, this is emptier than the new life. Now there is only the early spring night which is still as long as ever. Since I am living, I must make a fresh start. The first step is just to describe my remorse and grief, for Tzu-chun's sake as well as for my own.

All I can do is to cry. It sounds like a lilt as I mourn for Tzu-chun, burying her in oblivion.

I want to forget. For my own sake I don't want to remember the oblivion I gave Tzu-chun for her burial.

I must make a fresh start in life. I must hide the truth deep in my wounded heart, and advance silently, taking oblivion and falsehood as my guide. . . .

October 21, 1925

DING LING

WHEN I WAS IN XIA VILLAGE

■

Because of the turmoil in the Political Department, Comrade Mo Yü decided to send me to stay temporarily in a neighboring village. Actually, I was already completely well, but the opportunity to rest for a while in a quiet environment and arrange my notes from the past three months did have its attractions. So I agreed to spend two weeks in Xia Village, a place about ten miles from the Political Department.

A female comrade from the Propaganda Department, who was apparently on a work assignment, went with me. Since she wasn't a person who enjoyed conversation, however, the journey was rather lonely. Also, because her feet had once been bound and my own spirits were low, we traveled slowly. We set out in the morning, but it was nearly sunset by the time we reached our destination.

The village looked much like any other from a distance, but I knew it contained a very beautiful Catholic church that had escaped destruction and a small grove of pine trees. The place where I would be staying was in the midst of these trees, which clung to the hillside. From that spot it would be possible to look straight across to the church. By now I could see orderly rows of cave dwellings and the green trees above them. I felt content with the village.

My traveling companion had given me the impression that the village was very busy, but when we entered it, not even a single child or dog was to be seen. The only movement was dry leaves twirling about lightly in the wind. They would fly a short distance, then drop to earth again.

"This used to be an elementary school, but last year the Jap devils destroyed it. Look at those steps over there. That used to be a big classroom," my companion, Agui, told me. She was somewhat excited now, not so reserved as she had been during the day. Pointing to a large empty courtyard, she continued: "A year and a half ago, this area was full of life. Every evening after supper, the comrades gathered here to play soccer or basketball." Becoming more agitated, she asked, "Why isn't anyone here? Should we go to the assembly hall or head up the hill? We don't know where they've taken our luggage either. We have to straighten that out first."

On the wall next to the gate of the village assembly hall, many white paper slips had been pasted. They read "Office of the [Communist] Association," "Xia Village Branch of the [Communist] Association," and so on. But when we went inside, we couldn't find a soul. It was completely quiet, with only a few tables set about. We were both standing there dumbly when suddenly a man rushed in. He looked at us for a moment, seemed about to ask us something, but swallowed his words and prepared to dash away. We called to him to stop, however, and made him answer our questions.

"The people of the village? They've all gone to the west door. Baggage? Hmm. Yes, there was baggage. It was carried up the hill some time ago to Liu Erma's home." As he talked, he sized us up.

Learning that he was a member of the Peasant's Salvation Association, we asked him to accompany us up the hill and also asked him to deliver a note to one of the local comrades. He agreed to take the note, but he wouldn't go with us. He seemed impatient and ran off by himself.

The street too was very quiet. The doors of several shops were closed. Others were still open, exposing pitch-black interiors. We still couldn't find anyone. Fortunately, Agui was familiar with the village and led me up the hill. It was already dark. The winter sun sets very quickly.

The hill was not high, and a large number of stone cave dwellings were scattered here and there from the bottom to the top. In a few places, people were standing out in front peering into the distance. Agui knew very well that we had not yet reached our destination, but whenever we met someone she asked, "Is this the way to Liu Erma's house?" "How far is it to Liu Erma's house?" "Could you please tell me the way to Liu Erma's house?" Or, she would ask, "Did you notice any baggage being sent to Liu Erma's house? Is Liu Erma home?"

The answers we received always satisfied us, and this continued right up to the most distant and highest house, which was the Liu family's. Two small dogs were the first to greet us. Then a woman came out and asked who we were. As soon as they heard it was me, two more women came out. Holding a lantern, they escorted us into the courtyard and then into a cave on the side toward the east. The cave was virtually empty. On the *kang* under the window were piled my bedroll, my small leather carrying case, and Agui's quilt.

Some of the people there knew Agui. They took her hand and asked her many questions, and after a while they led her out, leaving me alone in the room. I arranged my bed and was about to lie down when suddenly they all crowded back in again. One of Liu Erma's daughters-in-law was carrying a bowl of noodles. Agui, Liu Erma, and a young girl were holding bowls, chopsticks, and a dish of onions and pepper. The young girl also brought in a brazier of burning coal.

Attentively, they urged me to eat some noodles and touched my hands and arms. Liu Erma and her daughter-in-law also sat down on the *kang*. There was an air of mystery about them as they continued the conversation interrupted by their entry into the room.

At first I thought I had caused their amazement, but gradually I realized that this wasn't the case. They were interested in only one thing—the topic of their conversation. Since all I heard were a few fragmentary sentences, I couldn't understand what they were talking about. This was especially true of what Liu Erma said because she frequently lowered her voice, as if afraid that someone might overhear her. Agui had changed completely. She now appeared quite capable and was very talkative. She listened closely to what the others were saying and seemed able to grasp the essence of their words. The daughter-in-law and the young girl said little. At times they added a word or two, but for the most part they just listened intently to what Agui and Liu Erma were saying. They seemed afraid to miss a single word.

Suddenly the courtyard was filled with noise. A large number of people had rushed in, and they all seemed to be talking at once. Liu Erma and the others climbed nervously off the *kang* and hurried outside. Without thinking, I followed along behind them to see what was happening.

By this time the courtyard was in complete darkness. Two red paper lanterns bobbed and weaved above the crowd. I worked my way into the throng and looked around. I couldn't see anything. The others also were squeezing in for no apparent reason. They seemed to want to say more, but they did not. I heard only simple exchanges that confused me even more.

"Yüwa, are you here too?"

"Have you seen her yet?"

"Yes, I've seen her. I was a little afraid."

"What is there to be afraid of? She's just a human being, and prettier than ever too."

At first I was sure that they were talking about a new bride, but people said that wasn't so. Then I thought there was a prisoner present, but that was wrong too. I followed the crowd to the doorway of the central cave, but all there was to see was more people packed tightly together. Thick smoke obscured my vision, so I had no choice but to back away. Others were also leaving by now, and the courtyard was much less crowded.

Since I couldn't sleep, I set about rearranging my carrying case by the lantern light. I paged through several notebooks, looked at photographs, and sharpened some pencils. I was obviously tired, but I also felt the kind of excitement that comes just before a new life begins. I prepared a time schedule for myself and was determined to adhere to it, beginning the very next day.

At that moment there was a man's voice at the door. "Are you asleep, comrade?" Before I could reply, the fellow entered the room. He was about twenty years old, a rather refined-looking country youth. "I received Director Mo's letter some time ago," he said. "This area is relatively quiet. Don't worry about a thing. That's my job. If you need something, don't hesitate to ask Liu Erma. Director Mo said you wanted to stay here for two weeks. Fine. If you enjoy your visit, we'd be happy to have you stay longer. I live in a neighboring cave, just below these. If you need me, just send someone to find me."

He declined to come up on the *kang*, and since there was no bench on the floor to sit on, I jumped down and said, "Ah! You must be Comrade Ma. Did you receive the note I sent you? Please sit down and talk for a while."

I knew that he held a position of some responsibility in the village. As a student he had not yet finished junior high school.

"They tell me you've written a lot of books," he responded. "It's too bad we haven't seen a single one." As he spoke he looked at my open carrying case that was lying on the *kang*. Our conversation turned to the subject of the local level of study. Then he said, "After you've rested for a few days, we'll definitely invite you to give a talk. It can be to a mass meeting or to a training class. In any case, you'll certainly be able to help us. Our most difficult task here is 'cultural recreation.'"

I had seen many young men like him at the Front. When I first met them, I was always amazed. I felt that these youth, who were somewhat remote from me, were really changing fast. Changing the subject, I asked him, "What was going on just now?"

"Zhenzhen, the daughter of Liu Dama, has returned," he answered. "I never thought she could be so great." I immediately sense a joyful, radiant twinkle in his eyes. As I was about to ask another question, he added, "She's come back from the Japanese area. She's been working there for over a year."

"Oh my!" I gasped.

He was about to tell me more when someone outside called for him. All he could say was that he'd be sure to have Zhenzhen call on me the next day. As if to provoke my interest further, he added that Zhenzhen must certainly have a lot of material for stories.

. . .

It was very late when Agui came back. She lay down on the *kang* but could not sleep. She tossed and turned and sighed continuously. I was very tired, but I still wished that she would tell me something about the events of the evening.

"No, comrade," she said. "I can't talk about it now. I'm too upset. I'll tell you tomorrow. Ahh . . . How miserable it is to be a woman." After this she covered her head with her quilt and lay completely still, no longer sighing. I didn't know when she finally fell asleep.

Early the next morning I stepped outside for a stroll, and before I knew it I had walked down to the village. I went into a general store to rest and buy red dates for Liu Erma to put in the rice porridge. As soon as the owner learned that I was living with Liu Erma, his small eyes narrowed and he asked me in a low, excited voice, "Did you get a look at her niece? I hear her disease has even taken her nose. That's because she was abused by the Jap devils." Turning his head, he called to his wife, who was standing in the inner doorway, "She has nerve, coming home! It's revenge against her father, Liu Fusheng."

"That girl was always frivolous. You saw the way she used to roam around the streets. Wasn't she Xia Dabao's old flame? If he hadn't been poor, wouldn't she have married him a long time ago?" As she finished speaking, the old woman lifted her skirts and came into the store.

The owner turned his face back toward me and said, "There are so many rumors." His eyes stopped blinking and his expression became very serious. "It's said that she has slept with at least a hundred men. Humph! I've heard that she even became the wife of a Japanese officer. Such a shameful woman should not be allowed to return."

Not wanting to argue with him, I held back my anger and left. I didn't look back, but I felt that he had again narrowed his small eyes and was feeling smug as he watched me walk away. As I neared the corner by the Catholic church, I overheard a conversation by two women who were drawing water at the well. One said, "She sought out Father Lu and told him she definitely wanted to be a nun. When Father Lu asked her for a reason, she didn't say a word, just cried. Who knows what she did there? Now she's worse than a prostitute . . ."

"Yesterday they told me she walks with a limp. Achh! How can she face people? Someone said she's even wearing a gold ring that a Jap devil gave her!"

"I understand she's been as far away as Datong and has seen many things. She can even speak Japanese."

My walk was making me unhappy, so I returned home. Since Agui had already gone out, I sat alone in my room and read a small pamphlet. After a while, I raised my eyes and noticed two large baskets for storing grain sitting near the wall. They must have had a long history, because they were as black as the wall itself. Opening the movable portion of the paper window, I peered out at the gray sky. The weather had changed completely from what it had been when I arrived a day before. The hard ground of the courtyard had been swept clean, and at the far edge a tree with a few withered branches stood out starkly against the leaden sky. There wasn't a single person to be seen.

I opened my carrying case, took out pen and paper, and wrote two letters. I wondered why Agui had not yet returned. I had forgotten that she had work to do. I was somehow thinking that she had come to be my companion. The days of winter are very short, but right then I was feeling that they were even longer than summer days.

Some time later, the young girl who had been in my room the night before came out into the courtyard. I immediately jumped down off the *kang*, stepped out the door, and called to her, but she just looked at me and smiled before rushing into another cave. I walked around the courtyard twice and then stopped to watch a hawk fly into the grove of trees by the church. The courtyard there had many large trees. I started walking again and, on the right side of the courtyard, picked up the sound of a woman crying. She was trying to stop, frequently blowing her nose.

I tried hard to control myself. I thought about why I was here and about all my plans. I had to rest and live according to the time schedule I had made. I returned to my room, but I couldn't sleep and had no interest in writing in my notebook.

Fortunately, a short while later Liu Erma came to see me. The young girl was with her, and her daughter-in-law arrived soon after. The three of them climbed up on the *kang* and took seats around the small brazier. The young girl looked closely at my things, which were laid out on the little square *kang* table.

"At that time no one could take care of anyone else," Liu Erma said, talking about the Japanese attack on Xia Village a year and a half before. "Those of us who lived on the hilltop were luckier. We could run away quickly. Many who lived in the village could not escape. Apparently it was all fate. Just then, on that day, our family's Zhenzhen had run over to the Catholic church. Only later did we learn that her unhappiness about what was happening had caused her to go to talk to the foreign priest about becoming a nun. Her father was in the midst of negotiating a marriage for her with the young proprietor of a rice store in Xiliu Village. He was almost thirty, a widower, and his family was well respected. We all said he would be a good match, but Zhenzhen said no and broke into tears before her father. In other matters, her father had always deferred to her wishes, but in this case the old man was adamant. He had no son and had always wanted to betroth his daughter to a good man. Who would have thought that Zhenzhen would turn around in anger and run off to the Catholic church. It was at that moment that the Japs caught her. How could her mother and father help grieving?"

"Was that her mother crying?"

"Yes."

"And your niece?"

"Well, she's really just a child. When she came back yesterday, she cried for a long time, but today she went to the assembly in high spirits. She's only eighteen."

"I heard she was the wife of a Japanese. Is that true?"

"It's hard to say. We haven't been able to find out for sure. There are many rumors, of course. She's contracted a disease, but how could anyone keep clean in such a place? The possibility of her marrying the merchant seems to be over. Who would want a woman who was abused by the Jap devils? She definitely has the disease. Last night she said so herself. This time she's changed a lot. When she talks about those devils, she shows no more emotion than if she were talking about an ordinary meal at home. She's only eighteen, but she has no sense of embarrassment at all."

"Xia Dabao came again today," the daughter-in-law said quietly, her questioning eyes fixed upon Erma.

"Who is Xia Dabao?" I asked.

"He's a young man who works in the village flour mill," replied Liu Erma. "When he was young, he and Zhenzhen were classmates for a year. They liked each other very much, but his family was poor, even poorer than ours. He didn't dare do anything, but our Zhenzhen was head over heels in love with him and kept clinging to him. Then she was upset when he didn't respond. Isn't it because of him that she wanted to be a nun? After Zhenzhen fell into the hands of the Jap devils, he often came to see her parents. At first just the sight of him made Zhenzhen's father angry. At times he cursed him, but Xia Dabao would say nothing. After a scolding he would leave and then come back another day. Dabao is really a good boy. Now he's even a squad leader in the self-defense corps. Today he came once again, apparently to talk with Zhenzhen's mother about marrying Zhenzhen. All I could hear was her crying. Later he left in tears himself."

"Does he know about your niece's situation?"

"How could he help knowing? There is no one in this village who doesn't know everything. They all know more than we do ourselves."

"Mother, everyone says that Xia Dabao is foolish," the young girl interjected.

"Humph! The boy has a good conscience. I approve of this match. Since the Jap devils came, who has any money? Judging from the words of Zhenzhen's parents, I think they approve too. If not him, who? Even without mentioning her disease, her reputation is enough to deter anyone."

"He was the one wearing the dark blue jacket and the copper-colored felt hat with the turned-up brim," the young girl said. Her eyes were sparkling with curiosity, and she seemed to understand this matter very well.

His figure began to take shape in my memory. When I went out for my walk earlier that morning, I had seen an alert, honest-looking young man who fit this description. He had been standing outside my courtyard, but had not shown any intention of coming in. On my way home, I had seen him again, this time emerging from the pine woods beyond the cave dwellings. I had thought he was someone from my courtyard or from a neighboring one and hadn't paid much attention to him. As I recalled him now, I felt that he was a rather capable man, not a bad young man at all.

I now feared that my plan for rest and recuperation could not be realized. Why were my thoughts so confused? I wasn't particularly anxious to meet anybody, and yet my mind still couldn't rest. Agui had come in during the conversation, and now she seemed to sense my feelings. As she went out with the others, she gave me a knowing smile. I understood her meaning and busied myself with arranging the *kang*. My bedroll, the lamp, and the fire all seemed much brighter. I had just placed the tea kettle on the fire when Agui returned. Behind her I heard another person.

"We have a guest, comrade!" Agui called. Even before she finished speaking, I heard someone giggling.

Standing in the doorway, I grasped the hands of this person whom I had not seen before. They were burning hot, and I couldn't help being a bit startled. She followed Agui up onto the *kang* and sat down. A single long braid hung down her back.

In the eyes of the new arrival, the cave that depressed me seemed to be something new and fresh. She looked around at everything with an excited glint in her eyes. She sat opposite me, her body tilted back slightly and her two hands spread apart on the bedroll for support. She didn't seem to want to say anything. Her eyes finally came to rest on my face.

The shadows lengthened her eyes and made her chin quite pointed. But even though her eyes were in deep shadow, her pupils shone brightly in the light of the lamp and the fire. They were like two open windows in a summer home in the country, clear and clean.

I didn't know how to begin a conversation without touching an open wound and hurting her self-respect. So my first move was to pour her a cup of hot tea.

It was Zhenzhen who spoke first: "Are you a Southerner? I think so. You aren't like the people from this province."

"Have you seen many Southerners?" I asked, thinking it best to talk about what she wanted to talk about.

"No," she said, shaking her head. Her eyes still fixed on me, she added, "I've only seen a few. They always seem a little different. I like you people from the South. Southern women, unlike us, can all read many, many books. I want to study with you. Will you teach me?"

I expressed my willingness to do so, and she quickly continued, "Japanese women also can read a lot of books. All those devil soldiers carried a few well-written letters, some from wives, some from girlfriends. Some were written by girls they didn't even know. They would include a photograph and use syrupy language. I don't know if those girls were sincere or not, but they always made the devils hold their letters to their hearts like precious treasures."

"I understand that you can speak Japanese," I said. "Is that true?"

Her face flushed slightly before she replied, in a very open manner, "I was there for such a long time. I went around and around for over a year. I can speak a fair amount. Being able to understand their language had many advantages."

"Did you go to a lot of different places with them?"

"I wasn't always with the same unit. People think that because I was the wife of a Jap officer I enjoyed luxury. Actually, I came back here twice before. Altogether, this is my third time. I was ordered to go on this last mission. There was no choice. I was familiar with the area, the work was important, and it was impossible to find anyone else in a short time. I won't be sent back anymore. They're going to treat my disease. That's fine with me because I've missed my dad and mom, and I'm glad to be able to come back to see them. My mother, though, is really hopeless. When I'm not home, she cries. When I'm here, she still cries."

"You must have known many hardships."

"She has endured unthinkable suffering," Agui interrupted, her face twisted in a pained expression. In a voice breaking with emotion, she added, "It's a real tragedy to be a woman, isn't it, Zhenzhen?" She slid over to be next to her.

"Suffering?" Zhenzhen asked, her thoughts apparently far, far away. "Right now I can't say for certain. Some things were hard to endure at the time, but when I recall them now they don't seem like much. Other things were no problem to do when I did them, but when I think about them now I'm very sad. More than a year . . . it's all past. Since I came back this time a great many people have looked at me strangely. As far as the people of this village are concerned, I'm an outsider. Some are very friendly to me. Others avoid me. The members of my family are just the same. They all like to steal looks at me. Nobody treats me the way they used to. Have I changed? I've thought about this a great deal, and I don't think I've changed at all. If I have changed, maybe it's that my heart has become somewhat harder. But could anyone spend time in such a place and not become hardhearted? People have no choice. They're forced to be like that!"

There was no outward sign of her disease. Her complexion was ruddy. Her voice was clear. She showed no signs of inhibition or rudeness. She did not exaggerate. She gave the impression that she had never had any complaints or sad thoughts. Finally, I could restrain myself no longer and asked her about her disease.

"People are always like that, even if they find themselves in worse situations. They brace themselves and see it through. Can you just give up and die? Later, after I made contact with our own people, I became less afraid. As I watched the Jap devils suffer defeat in battle and the guerrillas take action on all sides as a result of the tricks I was playing, I felt better by the day. I felt that even though my life was hard, I could still manage. Somehow I had to find a way to survive, and if at all possible, to live a life that was meaningful. That's why I'm pleased that they intend to treat my disease. It will be better to be cured. Actually, these past few days I haven't felt too bad. On the way home, I stayed in Zhangjiayi for two days and was given two shots and some medicine to take orally. The worst time was in the fall. I was told that my insides were rotting away, and then, because of some important information and the fact that no one could be found to take my place, I had to go back. That night I walked alone in the dark for ten miles. Every single step was painful. My mind was filled with the desire to sit down and rest. If the work hadn't been so important, I definitely wouldn't have gone back. But I had to. Ahh! I was afraid I might be recognized by the Jap devils, and I was also worried about missing my rendezvous. After it was over, I slept for a full week before I could pull myself together. It really isn't all that easy to die, is it?"

Without waiting for me to respond, she continued on with her story. At times she stopped talking and looked at us. Perhaps she was searching for reactions on our faces. Or maybe she was only thinking of something else. I could see that Agui was more troubled than Zhenzhen. For the most part she sat in silence, and when she did speak, it was only for a sentence or two. Her words gave voice to a limitless sympathy for Zhenzhen, but her expression when silent revealed even more clearly how moved she was by what Zhenzhen was saying. Her soul was being crushed. She herself was feeling the suffering that Zhenzhen had known before.

It was my impression that Zhenzhen had no intention whatever of trying to elicit sympathy from others. Even as others took upon themselves part of the misfortune that she had suffered, she seemed unaware of it. But that very fact made others feel even more sympathetic. It would have been better if, instead of listening to her recount the events of this period with a calmness that almost made you think she was talking about someone else, you could have heard her cry. Probably you would have cried with her, but you would have felt better.

After a while Agui began to cry, and Zhenzhen turned to comfort her. There were many things that I had wanted to discuss with Zhenzhen, but I couldn't bring myself to say anything. I wished to remain silent. After Zhenzhen left, I forced myself to read by the lamp for an hour. Not once did I look at Agui or ask her a question, even though she was lying very close to me, even though she tossed and turned and sighed all the time, unable to fall asleep.

After this Zhenzhen came to talk with me every day. She did not talk about herself alone. She very often showed great curiosity about many aspects of my life that were beyond her own experiences. At times, when my words were far removed from her life, it was obvious that she was struggling to understand, but nevertheless she listened intently. The two of us also took walks together down to the village. The youth were very good to her. Naturally, they were all activists. People like the owner of the general store, however, always gave us cold, steely stares. They disliked and despised Zhenzhen. They even treated me as someone not of their kind. This was especially true of the women, who, all because of Zhenzhen, became extremely self-righteous, perceiving themselves as saintly and pure. They were proud about never having been raped.

After Agui left the village, I grew even closer to Zhenzhen. It seemed that neither of us could be without the other. As soon as we were apart, we thought of each other. I like people who are enthusiastic and lively, who can be really happy or sad, and at the same time are straightforward and candid. Zhenzhen was just such a person. Our conversations took up a great deal of time, but I always felt that they were beneficial to my studies and to my personal growth. As the days went by, however, I discovered that Zhenzhen was not being completely open about something. I did not resent this. Moreover, I was determined not to touch upon this secret of hers. All people have things buried deeply in their hearts that they don't want to tell others. This secret was a matter of private emotions. It had nothing to do with other people or with Zhenzhen's own morality.

A few days before my departure, Zhenzhen suddenly began to appear very agitated. Nothing special seemed to have happened, and she showed no desire to talk to me about anything new. Yet she frequently came to my room looking disturbed and restless, and after sitting for a few minutes, she would get up and leave. I knew she had not eaten well for several days and was often passing up meals. I had asked her about her disease and knew that the cause of her uneasiness was not simply physical. Sometimes, after coming to my room, she would make a few disjointed remarks. At other times, she put on an attentive expression, as if asking me to talk. But I could see that her thoughts were elsewhere, on things that she didn't want others to know. She was trying to conceal her emotions by acting as if nothing was wrong.

Twice I saw that capable young man come out of Zhenzhen's home. I had already compared my impression of him with Zhenzhen, and I sympathized with him deeply. Zhenzhen had been abused by many men, and had contracted a stigmatized, hard-to-cure disease, but he still patiently came to see her and still sought the approval of her parents to marry her. He didn't look down on her. He did not fear the derision or the rebukes of others. He must have felt she needed him more than ever. He understood what kind of attitude a man should have toward the woman of his choice at such a time and what his responsibilities were.

But what of Zhenzhen? Although naturally there were many aspects of her emotions and her sorrows that I had not learned during this short period, she had never expressed any hope that a man would marry her or, if you will, comfort her. I thought she had become so hard because she had been hurt so badly. She seemed not to want anything from anyone. It would be good if love, some extraordinarily sympathetic commiseration, could warm her soul. I wanted her to find a place where she could cry this out. I was hoping for a chance to attend a wedding in this family. At the very least, I wanted to hear of an agreement to marry before I left.

"What is Zhenzhen thinking of?" I asked myself. "This can't be delayed indefinitely, and it shouldn't be turned into a big problem."

One day Liu Erma, her daughter-in-law, and her young daughter all came to see me. I was sure they intended to give me a report on something, but when they started to speak, I didn't allow them the opportunity to tell me anything. If my friend wouldn't confide in me, and I wouldn't ask her about it directly, then I felt it would be harmful to her, to myself, and to our friendship to ask others about it.

That same evening at dusk, the courtyard was again filled with people milling about. All the neighbors were there, whispering to one another. Some looked sad, but there were also those who appeared to find it all exciting. The weather was frigid, but curiosity warmed their hearts. In the severe cold, they drew in their shoulders, hunched their backs, thrust their hands into their sleeves, puffed out their breath, and looked at each other as if they were investigating something very interesting.

At first all I heard was the sound of quarreling coming from Liu Dama's dwelling. Then I heard Liu Dama crying. This was followed by the sound of a man crying. As far as I could tell, it was Zhenzhen's father. Next came a crash of dishes breaking. Unable to bear it any longer, I pushed my way through the curious onlookers and rushed inside.

"You've come at just the right time," Liu Erma said as she pulled me inside. "You talk to our Zhenzhen."

Zhenzhen's face was hidden by her long disheveled hair, but two wild eyes could still be seen peering out at the people gathered there. I walked over to her and stood beside her, but she seemed completely oblivious to my presence. Perhaps she took me as one of the enemy and not worth a moment's concern. Her appearance had changed so completely that I could hardly remember the liveliness, the bright pleasantness I had found in her before. She was like a cornered animal. She was like an evening goddess. Whom did she hate? Why was her expression so fierce?

"You're so heartless. You don't think about your mother

and father at all. You don't care how much I've suffered because of you in the last year." Liu Dama pounded on the *kang*
as she scolded her daughter, tears like raindrops dropping to
the *kang* or the floor and flowing down the contours of her
face. Several women had surrounded her and were preventing
her from coming down off the *kang*. It was frightening to see a
person lose her self-respect and allow all her feelings to come
out in a blind rage. I thought of telling her that such crying
was useless, but at the same time, I realized that nothing I
could say now would make any difference.

Zhenzhen's father looked very weak and old. His hands
hung down limply. He was sighing deeply. Xia Dabao was
seated beside him. There was a helpless look in his eyes as he
stared at the old couple.

"You must say something. Don't you feel sorry for your
mother?"

"When the end of a road is reached, one must turn. After water has flowed as far as it can, it must change direction.
Aren't you going to change at all? Why make yourself suffer?" The women were trying to persuade Zhenzhen with
such words.

I could see that this affair could not turn out the way
that everyone was hoping. Zhenzhen had shown me much
earlier that she didn't want anyone's sympathy. She, in turn,
had no sympathy for anyone else. She had made her decision
long ago and would not change. If people wanted to call
her stubborn, then so be it. With teeth tightly clenched, she
looked ready to stand up to all of them.

At last the others agreed to listen to me, and I asked Zhenzhen to come to my room and rest. I told them that everything could be discussed later that night. But when I led Zhenzhen out of the house, she did not follow me to my room. Instead, she ran off up the hillside.

"That girl has big ideas."

"Humph! She looks down on us country folk."

"She's such a cheap little hussy and yet she puts on such airs. Xia Dabao deserves it . . ."

These were some of the comments being made by the crowd in the courtyard. Then, when they realized that there was no longer anything of interest to see, the crowd drifted away.

I hesitated for a while in the courtyard before deciding to go up the hillside myself. On the top of the hill were numerous graves set among the pine trees. Broken stone tablets stood before them. No one was there. Not even the sound of a falling leaf broke the stillness. I ran back and forth calling Zhenzhen's name. What sounded like a response temporarily comforted my loneliness, but in an instant the vast silence of the hills became even deeper. The colors of the sunset had completely faded. All around me a thin, smoke-like mist rose silently and spread out to the middle slopes of the hills, both nearby and in the distance. I was worried and sat down weakly on a tombstone. Over and over I asked myself, "Should I go on up the hill or wait for her here?" I was hoping that I could relieve Zhenzhen of some of her distress.

At that moment I saw a shadow moving toward me from below. I quickly saw that it was Xia Dabao. I remained silent, hoping that he wouldn't see me and would continue on up the hill, but he came straight at me. At last I felt that I had to greet him and called, "Have you found her? I still haven't seen her."

He walked over to me and sat down on the dry grass. He said nothing, only stared into the distance. I felt a little uneasy. He really was very young. His eyebrows were long and thin. His eyes were quite large, but now they looked dull and lifeless. His small mouth was tightly drawn. Perhaps before it had been appealing, but now it was full of anguish, as if trying to hold in his pain. He had an honest-looking nose, but of what use was it to him now?

"Don't be sad," I said. "Maybe tomorrow everything will be all right. I'll talk to her this evening."

"Tomorrow, tomorrow—she'll always hate me. I know that she hates me." He spoke in a sad low voice that was slightly hoarse.

"No," I replied, searching my memory. "She has never shown me that she hates anyone." This was not a lie.

"She wouldn't tell you. She wouldn't tell anyone. She won't forgive me as long as she lives."

"Why should she hate you?"

"Of course—" he began. Suddenly he turned his face toward me and looked at me intently. "Tell me," he said, "at that time I had nothing. Should I have encouraged her to run away with me? Is all of this my fault? Is it?"

He didn't wait for my answer. As if speaking to himself, he went on, "It is my fault. Could anyone say that I did the right thing? Didn't I bring this harm to her? If I had been as brave as she, she never would have—I know her character. She'll always hate me. Tell me, what should I do? What would she want me to do? How can I make her happy? My life is worthless. Am I of even the slightest use to her? Can you tell me? I simply don't know what I should do. Ahhh! How miserable things are! This is worse than being captured by the Jap devils." Without a break, he continued to mumble on and on.

When I asked him to go back home with me, he stood up and we took several steps together. Then he stopped and said that he had heard a sound coming from the very top of the hill. There was nothing to do but encourage him to go on up, and I watched until he had disappeared into the thick pines. Then I started back. By now it was almost completely dark. It was very late when I went to bed that night, but I still hadn't received any news. I didn't know what had happened to them.

Even before I ate breakfast the next morning, I finished packing my suitcase. Comrade Ma had promised that he would be coming this day to help me move, and I was all prepared to return to the Political Department and then go on to [my next assignment]. The enemy was about to start another "mopping-up campaign," and my health would not permit me to remain in this area. Director Mo had said that the ill definitely had to be moved out first, but I felt uneasy.

Should I try to stay? If I did, I could be a burden to others. What about leaving? If I went, would I ever be able to return? As I was sitting on my bedroll pondering these questions, I sensed someone slipping quietly into my room.

With a single thrust of her body, Zhenzhen jumped up onto the *kang* and took a seat opposite me. I could see that her face was slightly swollen, and when I grasped her hands as she spread them over the fire, the heat that had made such an impression on me before once again distressed me. Then and there I realized how serious her disease was.

"Zhenzhen," I said, "I'm about to leave. I don't know when we'll meet again. I hope you'll listen to your mother—"

"I have come to tell you," she interrupted, "that I'll be leaving tomorrow too. I want to leave home as soon as possible."

"Really?" I asked.

"Yes," she said, her face again revealing that special vibrancy. "They've told me to go in for medical treatment."

"Ah," I sighed, thinking that perhaps we could travel together. "Does your mother know?"

"No, she doesn't know yet. But if I say that I'm going for medial treatment and that after my disease is cured I'll come back, she'll be sure to let me go. Just staying at home doesn't have anything to offer, does it?"

At this moment I felt that she had a rare serenity about her. I recalled the words that Xia Dabao had spoken to me the previous evening and asked her directly, "Has the problem of your marriage been resolved?"

"Resolved? Oh, well, it's all the same."

"Did you heed your mother's advice?" I still didn't dare express my hopes for her. I didn't want to think of the image left in my mind by that young man. I was hoping that someday he would be happy.

"Why should I listen to what they say? Did they ever listen to me?"

"Well, are you really angry with them?"

There was no response.

"Well, then, do you really hate Xia Dabao?"

For a long time she did not reply. Then, in a very calm voice, she said, "I can't say that I hate him. I just feel now that I'm someone who's diseased. It's a fact that I was abused by a large number of Jap devils. I don't remember the exact number. In any case, I'm unclean, and with such a black mark I don't expect any good fortune to come my way. I feel that living among strangers and keeping busy would be better than living at home where people know me. Now that they've approved sending me to [Yan'an] for treatment, I've been thinking about staying there and doing some studying. I hear it's a big place with lots of schools and that anyone can attend. It's better for each of us to go our own separate ways than it is to have everyone stay together in one place. I'm doing this for myself, but I'm also doing it for the others. I don't feel that I owe anyone an apology. Neither do I feel especially happy. What I feel is that after I go to [Yan'an], I'll be in a new situation. I will be able to start life fresh. A person's life is not just for one's father and mother, or even for oneself. Some have called me young, inexperienced, and bad-tempered. I don't dispute it. There are some things that I just have to keep to myself."

I was amazed. Something new was coming out of her. I felt that what she had said was really worth examining. There was nothing for me to do but express approval of her plan.

When I took my departure, Zhenzhen's family was there to see me off. She, however, had gone to the village office. I didn't see Xia Dabao before I left either.

I wasn't sad as I went away. I seemed to see the bright future that Zhenzhen had before her. The next day I would be seeing her again. That had been decided. And we would still be together for some time. As soon as Comrade Ma and I walked out the door of Zhenzhen's home, he told me of her decision and confirmed that what she had told me that morning would quickly come to pass.

Translated by Gary J. Bjorge